A WOMAN SCORNED

JAMES HENEGHAN

RAVEN BOOKS
an imprint of
ORCA BOOK PUBLISHERS

Library and Archives Canada Cataloguing in Publication

Heneghan, James, 1930-
A woman scorned / James Heneghan.
(Rapid reads)

Issued also in electronic formats.
ISBN 978-1-4598-0406-7

I. Title. II. Series: Rapid reads
PS8565.E58IW66 2013   C813'.54   C2013-901927-8

First published in the United States, 2013
Library of Congress Control Number: 2013904966

Summary: When a prominent city councilor turns up dead in his posh
condo, the police are content to call it suicide. But reporter Sebastian Casey
thinks otherwise and sets out to prove it on his own. (RL 4.5)

MIX
Paper from
responsible sources
FSC® C016245

*Orca Book Publishers is dedicated to preserving the environment and has
printed this book on Forest Stewardship Council® certified paper.*

Orca Book Publishers gratefully acknowledges the support for
its publishing programs provided by the following agencies:
the Government of Canada through the Canada Book Fund and the
Canada Council for the Arts, and the Province of British Columbia
through the BC Arts Council and the Book Publishing Tax Credit.

Design by Teresa Bubela
Cover photography by Getty Images

ORCA BOOK PUBLISHERS   ORCA BOOK PUBLISHERS
PO Box 5626, Stn. B   PO Box 468
Victoria, BC Canada   Custer, WA USA
V8R 6S4   98240-0468

www.orcabook.com
Printed and bound in Canada.

16 15 14 13 • 4 3 2 1

For my family:
Ann, Robert, John, Leah, Margaux, Lee, Arran,
Rebecca, Hank, Ruth and Bethiah.

And for Lucy, as always.

Heaven has no rage, like love to hatred turned,
Nor hell a fury, like a woman scorned.

—WILLIAM CONGREVE, *THE MOURNING BRIDE*

1697

1

Rain and blustering winds pounded the West End. Muddy pink blossoms littered the streets and clogged the drains. April was always an unpredictable month in Vancouver.

It was Sunday morning. In the luxury penthouse suite of the Roosevelt Building overlooking Stanley Park, a man and a woman were finishing breakfast. The man had eaten hardly a thing, merely pushing the food around his plate. Finally he put down his knife and fork.

"I'm moving out, Moira," he said quietly.

The woman stared. "What?"

"I've already packed a few things. I'll be gone by noon."

He was forty-four-year-old Vancouver City Councilor George Hamilton Nash. Slim from regular exercise, he had a narrow face, brown eyes and dark hair. He was wearing his black Lacoste bathrobe and tartan slippers.

His wife, Moira, forty-three, had pale skin and gray eyes. She wore her dark hair short to the jawline. On Friday her hairdresser had taken care of the advancing gray, adding several blond highlights. She seldom wore makeup before breakfast.

High-school sweethearts, they had been married for twenty-one years.

There were no children.

"Moving out? I don't understand," she said. She became agitated, pushing back her chair. Her table napkin fell to the floor. "Moving where?"

"Not far. I bought a condo in the Shangri-La Hotel."

"You're leaving me?"

"Don't think of it that way, Moira. I'm not leaving you. I just won't live here anymore. My new place is less than ten blocks from here. I'll be very close."

"But why? I don't get it."

"I don't expect you to get it, Moira, but I want to live my own life. I've been thinking of this for a long time. I need to be alone. I need to explore new things. New life experiences."

"Life experiences? You've gone mad!"

"I knew you wouldn't understand. Look—I've lived with someone all my life. First it was my parents. Then when I went to college I had roommates. Then I met you and we got married. Twenty years we've been together—"

"Twenty-one."

"—and I've never lived alone. I'm forty-four years old, Moira. My life is half over and I've never known what it's like to live alone. In complete freedom."

"So it's freedom you want, is it? I know what you're up to, George. It's all those young women at city hall. Making eyes at handsome City Councilor George Hamilton Nash. They even call you at home. Your slutty city-hall clerks," she said angrily. "Don't try to deny it. I can pick up the phone in the bedroom and hear you talking to them from your study. I'm not stupid."

"Spying on me. Exactly why I need to move out."

"How can you talk of leaving?" she said, shaking her head in disbelief. "I need you here with me, George. My surgery is next week. You know that very well." She stood and faced him across the table. "Wait. Just wait till I can manage on my own. Until I'm back on my feet and we've had a chance to discuss everything. A few weeks at least."

He shook his head.

She started to weep. "George will never leave me, I always tell myself. George is strong. George is good. How wrong I was! Casting me off like an old sweater. How can you do this, George?" Her weeping grew in intensity.

He threw down his napkin and bounded up from the table.

"Wait!" she said. "Come back here!" She hurried after him, clawing at his back. He tried to shrug her off, but she clung to him, her nails buried in his bathrobe. "You will regret this, you bastard," she screamed.

He shoved her violently, and she fell to the floor.

"You'll be sorry," she said between sobs.

He marched into his study and locked the door.

It would be good to be rid of her, he thought. He should have left years ago. Live his own life. Do whatever he wanted. A free agent.

No wet blanket of a wife to slow him down. His new luxury condo was on the fortieth floor. Views of the yacht club, ocean and mountains.

Alone. Sweet word. With occasional guests. He grinned at the thought.

Moira hammered his door with her fists and then collapsed to her knees. After a while, she got up and made her way to the bathroom. She swallowed several pills and then lay on their unmade bed, eyes closed.

She didn't hear him go.

Some time later, still in her housecoat, she paced furiously about their apartment. Eventually she crumpled into a loveseat near the high windows. She looked out. Wind and rain swept over a deserted Stanley Park. Tall cedars, firs and hemlocks swayed together in a wild spring dance.

She bent her head and sobbed into her clenched fists.

2

Sebastian Casey made his way home Friday evening after a light day's work.

Light work suited him fine. Casey was not an ambitious man, seeking neither fame nor fortune. He lived and worked in the busy West End. He was a journalist, six years now with the *West End Clarion*, a small-circulation weekly newspaper. The ten years he'd spent with a regular big-city newspaper had been enough. Too busy. Too demanding. For Casey, life came first, work a distant second.

Casey's small eighth-floor Barclay Street apartment was only a few blocks from the *Clarion* office.

Surrounded on three sides by the sea, the West End district covered an area of roughly one square mile. To the north were the high snowy mountains. Seen from Casey's apartment on a fine day they could have been the Swiss Alps.

He poured himself a Jameson Irish whiskey and soda over ice in a tall glass. Carried it over to the small balcony outside his slider window and looked down at the street. Not many people about. Quiet. Faintly greening horse-chestnut trees. A squirrel was scratching about in Matty Kayle's front yard over on the other side of the street.

The whiskey started a warm glow of contentment in his bones.

He finished his drink and took a leisurely shower. Stood on his bathroom scales. Checked his image in the mirror. Sleepy blue eyes. Hair the color of red sandstone. Since meeting Emma Shaughnessy last November, he had met his goal of dropping twenty pounds. She'd suggested he stop buying his clothes at thrift shops. Patronize a proper menswear shop instead. After she gave him a makeover, he looked smarter, slimmer. Best of all, he felt fit. He owed it all to Emma.

He missed her. Looked forward to her regular Sunday call from Ireland.

At the beginning of March, Casey and Emma had taken an Irish holiday together. They'd thought of it as a honeymoon, though there had been no formal marriage. They didn't mind the Irish rain. It was softer and more forgiving than the Canadian kind. Its molecules had greened over eight hundred years of Irish sorrow and suffering. They stayed a week at the cozy bed-and-breakfast home of Mrs. Bridie Mulligan in Dublin, on the River Liffey.

After that they rented a car and drove west to another bed-and-breakfast in Galway, on the River Corrib. This one was the home of Mrs. Annie Gallagher, a cheerful, pink-faced woman of comfortable girth. After a week with Mrs. Gallagher, they drove to Derry, in the north, to Emma's old home.

Emma was shocked to find her mother ailing. Over ninety years old, Mrs. Shaughnessy was thin and feeble. She was alone and getting weaker. Though she wrote to Emma regularly, she'd never complained of illness. Emma's father had passed away years ago, so there was no one else.

Neighbors had helped by moving the old lady's bed down to the living room. For months the doctor had been trying to persuade her to move into a nursing home, but she had refused to go.

Emma had called the Vancouver School Board and arranged a leave of absence so she could stay and take care of her mother.

Casey had returned to Vancouver alone.

That was a month ago.

Now, he wrapped himself in his dressing gown and mixed himself another drink.

The whiskey beside him, he settled into his comfortable armchair for an hour of reading. Then he would throw on his raincoat and go out for something to eat. Probably to the new sushi house only two blocks away on Denman.

* * *

Sunday.

Casey relished his Sundays. In the morning he usually walked or jogged the Stanley Park seawall. In the afternoon he relaxed, reading magazines and newspapers. The evening was for *Masterpiece Theatre* on PBS or for reading.

But right now, after his seawall walk, he was looking forward to two o'clock and Emma's phone call. Ten at night back in Ireland. He poured himself an Irish whiskey and soda over ice in a tall glass. It was almost two. He was ready.

When the phone rang, he picked up. "Casey," he said.

"Hello, Casey."

"I miss you, Emma."

"I miss you too," Emma said.

"How's your mother?"

"She won't get well. Ma knows it. She's worn out and ready to go. I will stay with her to the end and do what I can to ease it for her."

"I want you back," Casey said. "I'm no good without you."

"Casey, I have a confession to make."

Casey said nothing.

"This is hard to tell," Emma said in a low voice.

"So tell," Casey said, his stomach tightening.

"You remember John Burns?"

Casey said nothing.

"You met him when you were here. John and I were at university together. I went out with him for a short time back in those days. He teaches at Queen's, in Belfast, remember?"

He remembered John Burns all right.

An imposter of a man.

Emma had introduced Casey to him one evening at John Burns's book-signing event. A bookshop on Fountain Street, in Belfast. Burns had published a book of Irish literary criticism. After the signing, Burns had taken them to his favorite bar for a drink. They found a seat away from the television. Casey bought the drinks.

Burns liked the sound of his own voice. He directed his talk mainly at Emma, while Casey sat and listened. Burns dropped names of famous Irish writers, Man Booker prizewinners. They were his friends. There was Colm Tóibín, whom John Burns called "Toby." Then there was John Banville, or "Johnny."

"I was talking to Roddy at the Guinness Peat Awards in Dublin not so long ago," Burns said, "and he was telling me about a small problem with his WIP."

"Roddy Doyle?" Emma said.

Burns nodded.

Emma looked impressed.

"What's WIP?" Casey said.

"Work-in-progress," Burns said to Emma.

Casey had excused himself. He'd stared at the glossy white toilet tiles in front of his eyes.

"Johnny Banville, how are ye?" he'd said aloud.

But the white tiles had made no reply.

Now, on the phone with Emma, Casey could say nothing. His throat seemed suddenly congested.

"Casey?" Emma said. "Are you there?"

"I'm here," Casey said with difficulty.

"Well, John and I started keeping company," Emma said quietly.

"Does 'keeping company' mean the same as sleeping together?" Casey said.

Silence.

"I didn't mean for it to happen," Emma said after a while. "But it did. What can I say? I still love you just as much as ever, Casey, I swear. But I had to tell you. I want no secrets between us."

Casey couldn't speak.

"Are you there, Casey? Say something."

"I don't have anything to say, Emma."

"Nothing?" Emma said.

"Only that I love you and want you back," Casey said. "I'm waiting for you."

He hung up the phone and mixed a second whiskey and soda in a very tall glass. With lots of ice.

3

One of Casey's main jobs at the *West End Clarion* was covering council meetings at city hall, following up on stories of interest to

West End residents. He knew the councilors personally from frequent face-to-face interviews.

Today he had an appointment with Councilor George Hamilton Nash in his office, just before the council meeting.

Nash stood up from behind his desk to greet him. They shook hands. "Take a seat, Casey," he said. "What can I do for you?"

Nash was a successful businessman and councilor. Casey had never warmed to the man. He didn't know why. All he could say in the councilor's favor was that he was a sharp dresser. Today he wore an expensive gray suit, white shirt, blue tie, black loafers.

"Word on the street, councilor, is you're planning to run for the mayor's job in November," Casey said.

Nash's eyes glittered. "Sorry to disappoint you, Casey. Man in your profession shouldn't be paying any attention to rumors."

"More than a rumor, George. The smart boys at the Vancouver Club are in your corner. They seem to think you'd be a sure thing."

Nash shrugged. "I'll level with you, Casey, but this is off the record, okay?"

"Off the record, councilor."

"I can tell you nothing till I've had a chance to see what kind of support I can count on. If I get the support, then I might have an announcement to make. All I can say, okay?"

"You think you'd make a good mayor, George?"

"You know damn right I would, Casey."

* * *

The city council meeting, on the third floor of city hall, had been in session for an hour. Casey was doing his best to stay awake. Late to bed last night and too much whiskey had drained his energy. Couldn't think. Except for the image of Emma having sex with John Burns. He was destroyed with jealousy when he thought of the two of them doing it together.

Now he was wide awake. Jealousy and lethargy mixed about as well as oil and water.

He peered over the top of the city-hall media desk at Mayor Bronson. His ten council members sat in an arc across the width of the chamber. There were several women on council. Two more women, City Clerk Barbara Scott and Council Secretary Margaret Mullen, sat at desks one level below the councilors.

The council chambers were two stories high. Four chandeliers. High windows partially curtained to diminish the light. Walls of dark walnut veneer. The chamber had a gallery built to hold a hundred people. Today it was empty.

Like Casey.

He thought again of Emma.

His Emma.

Emma and John Burns doing it together.

Where? Up at the university in Burns's narrow bed? Or upstairs in her mother's old house? Or lying together in the heather? Copulating like rabbits behind the fuchsia hedges? That self-satisfied little nobody. With his book of literary criticism. And his Roddys and his Johnnys and his Tobys.

He vowed to think no more of upstart John Burns.

The media desk was long enough to accommodate eight reporters. Today, only Casey and a man from *The Province* were there. It was late. The mayor and his councilors were discussing a thirty-two-page report.

The topic was backyard hens. Vancouver residents would be allowed up to four hens in their backyards. Councilors raised questions. Backyard hens would cause smells, noise, disease, rats and who knows what else? And what would be done about hens wandering from backyards and getting lost? Wandering into traffic? Causing accidents?

There were answers. The culture around urban farming was changing. Sustainable agriculture was the way of the future. As for wandering chickens, or lost chickens, or abandoned chickens, the mayor's idea was to spend $20,000 on a home for homeless chickens. An obvious solution. This proposal ruffled more than a few feathers as the debate heated up. There were other questions: Would roosters be allowed or would it be just hens? What about ducks, turkeys and geese? Cries of "Fowl!" in the council chamber.

"Isn't it enough," cried one councilor, leaping to his feet, "that the city is now known as Vansterdam for providing free marijuana to drug addicts? And free booze to alcoholics?

Now the mayor wants to provide a free home for lost chickens!"

Another idea of the mayor's was that Vancouver citizens be encouraged to dig up their lawns and grow wheat or potatoes. It was called "sustainable food growth."

It was much better for his peace of mind, Casey decided, to think about the problems of homeless chickens and sustainable potatoes than to dwell on what might or might not be going on between Emma and John Burns.

Councilor George Nash took very little part in the debate. He sat back in his chair, relaxed, smiling occasionally to himself. But contributing very little. Beside him, Councilor Angela Brill made up for Nash's silence by speaking often. An attractive blond woman in her thirties, she regarded her fellow councilors with ill-disguised disdain.

Casey secretly agreed with Councilor Brill, who had declared both topics—homeless chickens and obsolete lawns—tiresome and absurd. These were matters of little concern to the majority of taxpayers, she argued.

Homeless chickens should never have found their way onto the agenda, she said.

"It's all really quite eggstrordinary," one of the other councilors complained.

Except for Councilor George Nash, nobody laughed at the clever pun.

Taxpayers were starting to call city hall Silly Hall, another councilor said.

Enough for today. Casey could take no more Silly Hall. Besides, it was late. He left the council chamber, ignored the elevator and took the stairs down to the street.

A light rain.

What did Emma and her literary lover do when it rained in Ireland? Did they drive to a hotel in nearby Ballymagowan for a bally good time?

Casey tugged his old tweed cap from the pocket of his new Burberry raincoat and pulled it over his brick-red hair. He had bought the cap many years ago in a Donegal market and wasn't about to give it up, even for Emma. It kept him in touch with his native Ireland. A sentimental fancy, he knew.

He stood in the rain at the bus stop beside a man wearing trendy rain gear from the local outdoors store.

"Bloody rain," the man said.

"Soft," Casey said, his mind in Ireland. "Falling soft."

The man turned his back on him.

In twenty minutes, Casey was back in the West End. Sitting at the bar in O'Doul's, sipping his first whiskey of the day.

When he emerged onto Robson Street a short time later, the rain had stopped.

Brenda at the front desk of the *Clarion* was getting ready to go home. She smiled when she saw him. "Two messages for you, Casey."

Brenda was young, still in her twenties. Medium build, blond hair, hazel eyes. She looked nice in her cream blouse and gray pantsuit. Brenda was smart, friendly and efficient. She was the newspaper's public face and sometime contributor to the *Clarion's* pop music column.

"Thanks, Brenda." Casey glanced at the two yellow slips before tossing them into Brenda's wastepaper bin.

"Debbie still here?" Casey said.

"Went home fifteen minutes ago," Brenda said.

Debbie Ozeroff covered the arts, fashion, environment and women's issues. She and Casey shared an office the size of a postage stamp. They also shared duties when things got too busy.

"Goodnight, Casey," Brenda said.

"See you tomorrow, Brenda."

Casey typed up his city hall report and then left. The rain was keeping off. He walked home amid spring's heady smells. Rain, earth, trees and flowers.

4

A month had gone by since Councilor George Hamilton Nash had walked out on his wife.

On Wednesday, he left his office just after five and started walking home along Beach Avenue at English Bay. The first two weeks of May had been mostly fine. Sun and clouds. Sparkling slate-green sea. Red rhododendrons and bright yellow and purple azaleas provided a colorful background to Vancouver's latest work of art—fourteen giant bronze sculptures in Morton Park. The figures were frozen in convulsions of laughter. But Nash wasn't laughing. Worried about business, he failed to notice either the beauty or the humor of his surroundings.

One of his companies, Oasis Investments, was handled by his longtime partner Joanne Drummond. In their meeting an hour earlier, they had argued about the business and the way Joanne was handling it.

Business partners for over fifteen years, it had been their first serious argument.

George and Joanne had met as UBC students many years ago. They'd begun an irregular sexual relationship that had lasted right up to the present day. Joanne had never married. Their business relationship was more robust than their sexual one. A pretty, slightly plump woman, Joanne enjoyed all the good things that life had to offer.

But Nash was now deeply concerned. Drummond had become a big spender over the past year. First it was a three-bedroom home in

Vancouver's high-end Kitsilano district. That had to be worth a million and a half. Then she bought a "cute" waterfront cottage on Gambier Island. Not much less. To top it off, she'd recently gone out and bought herself a new BMW sports car. All this within the space of one year. Business was good, but not that good, Nash decided.

He had let himself into Joanne's office late one night and examined a small sample of her client portfolios. The more he searched, the more worried he became. She was cheating. There was no other word for it. As far as Nash could see, Joanne had been mishandling clients for at least two years. She had been enriching herself at the expense of the company and its clients. Today he had confronted her.

"I'm keeping my clients happy," Joanne argued.

"But you can't offer clients a steady fifteen-to-twenty-percent return, Joanne. Where will the money come from?"

"From new clients."

Nash threw up his hands. "You can't pay clients with their own money. Or with money from new clients. What the hell do you think you're doing, Jo? It's called fraud. You want to pay constant high returns? Then you need an ever-increasing flow of cash from new investors. I'm not telling you anything you don't know. It's a Ponzi scheme, pure and simple. What the hell were you thinking?"

"No, it's not. Not the way I'm running it. You're exaggerating—"

"How long do you think you can keep it going, Joanne? One year? Two? Maybe three? What do we do when the tsunami comes? If our earnings are less than payments to our clients, we're done for. The tsunami sweeps us away. The system collapses. You know that, Joanne. What the hell made you think—?"

"George, you worry too much. If you leave everything to me you'll see—"

"I don't plan to leave everything to you, Joanne. Not anymore. You're finished. You want the pair of us to end up in prison? I won't let you do it. You leave me no choice but to report it to the police."

"Don't even think of it, George!"

"Just you watch me, Jo!"

* * *

Sunday afternoon. Two o'clock Vancouver time. Ten o'clock in Belfast.

Casey waited, a whiskey and soda beside the telephone. His first today. Emma hadn't called last week. He wondered if his phone would be silent again today.

But it rang. Right on time.

"Casey? It's me, Emma."

"It's good to hear your voice, Emma."

"It's good to hear yours, Casey. I'm sorry I missed last week. I fell asleep reading to Ma in front of the fire. How are you? Are you keeping up with your gym workouts? And your jogs on the seawall?"

"I am. What about you?"

"I'm the same. Nothing ever changes here, except Ma. She won't last much longer, I'm afraid. All she does is sleep. Father Grafton performed last rites yesterday, and the neighbors came in to pray. I made sausage rolls and shortbread for everyone to go with the whiskey."

"You sound tired," Casey said.

"I am so," Emma said. "It's late here. Everyone is in bed by ten. I miss my runs in

Stanley Park. I miss them terribly. But this morning I managed to get away for a gallop in the glen. Annie Murphy came in and sat with Ma."

Silence.

"You're not saying much, Casey. Are you sure you're all right?"

"I'm all right," Casey said. "I'm not one for chatter, you know that well enough."

"I do. I still think of you as 'the quiet man.' I miss that quietness of yours. I'd give anything to have you here with me. To come walking in the narrow lanes and see the wild fuchsia hedges ablaze with purple and red. It's lovely here right now."

"Is it lovely for your friend John Burns? Do you take him walking through the lanes of red-and-purple fuchsia?"

"Oh, Casey, please! Don't spoil things. I love you. You're the only one. It won't be long before I'm home, yours again. You'll see. Don't be bitter. Emma Shaughnessy is no saint. She's just a woman. She makes mistakes. But she loves you, Casey. Please believe that."

"You're right, Emma. The devil's in me sometimes. I'm waiting for you."

"I'm for bed," Emma said. "Say a prayer for us."

"That'd be you and me?"

"That'd be right."

"Then I will," Casey said.

He hung up the phone, poured himself a second whiskey and soda and sat for a while, thinking. Beyond his job and beyond his colleagues at the office, Casey lived in a deep silence. This silence often tightened around him and almost smothered him. It was why he needed Emma. To bring air and color and sound to his life. It was why he sometimes spent an hour alone in the noise and clatter of O'Doul's bar.

He wouldn't be himself until she was back with him in Vancouver once again.

5

She let herself in to Nash's apartment with her key and was waiting for him when he got home. Naked on the bed, lying on her side, one milk-white hip thrust up in a perfect arc.

Leaning on one elbow, a magazine partially hiding one plump breast. Enticing smile. Two drinks waiting on the night table.

He threw off his clothes and slipped into bed beside her.

The digital clock on the bedside table read 6:35 PM, *Wednesday, May 23*.

She turned to him eagerly. Her magazine fell to the floor.

She was on something, he could tell. That smile. Something in the eyes, something wild. He reached out to her, fondling her breasts.

She giggled and wriggled away. "Just wait and see what I've got for you."

He watched her glide naked across the carpeted floor. At the foot of the bed she picked up a large handbag. From it she took several silk ropes.

Ropes. Good. He liked it when she steered the ship.

She carefully tied his wrists to the bedposts with two lengths of the rope. They had played this game before, but these fancy ropes were something new.

"No handcuffs today?" George said.

"Not this time. Last time we played this game, they left marks on your wrists. You will find this more comfortable. Now move down in the bed so your arms are stretched."

He wriggled down.

"Spread your legs, darling," she whispered, kissing his toes.

He obeyed, and she tied his ankles to the bottom posts. Then she bit the toe she had just kissed. Bit it hard.

"Arrgh!" George screamed.

While his mouth was open, she gagged him. Quickly stuffing one of his socks into his mouth as far as it would go.

He shook his head wildly. What was going on? Was she mad? She had never done anything like this before. The sounds in his throat sounded to his own ears like animal noises. He struggled but couldn't free himself. He tried to cry out but could make very little noise. Tried to spit the gag out, but she pressed a strip of duct tape across his mouth, over the sock.

She pulled up a chair and sat beside his head, looking into his eyes. She was still naked.

"Now comes the best part, George," she said. Her intimate smile was gone. Eyes spinning with excitement.

She held a twelve-inch butcher knife in front of his eyes. He could see it clearly. Excellent quality. Expensive. From his own kitchen.

He'd known that tonight she was different. He had been a fool to let her tie him up.

She gently tested the blade of the knife on his arm. Sharp like a razor. Blood, bright red, leaping to the surface of his skin. He struggled. He fought. He kicked. He wrestled.

In vain.

"Just one more cut," she said. "That's all. But deep enough this time to finish you off. I'm here to watch you die, George. You miserable excuse for a man. You know how much I hate infidelity."

She was slurring her words.

He jerked his arms as hard as he could, but the ropes and bedposts held. He tried to scream, but the gag silenced him.

She was holding the knife in front of his face again.

A tiny drop of his blood shone on the bright knife edge.

He squeezed his eyes closed as he felt the blade slice into his flesh. He howled behind the gag as the blood flowed down his arm and onto the bed.

She sat back, watching.

She was talking, but he could not understand a word. He sucked air in through his nostrils. His heart pounded. His blood flowed.

"Minutes. That's all you have left of life, George. Minutes."

He knew she was right. He knew he was dying. She was mad. But he couldn't stop her. The crazy bitch was killing him. He watched the blood. Then he closed his eyes. It wasn't something he'd thought much about before— blood. He was dying because he couldn't stop her from stealing his blood, emptying his life onto the bed.

He was still young. To die with so much more living left in him was a terrible waste. There was so much he'd wanted to do. So much.

Too late now.

This was death. This was how it felt.

She was talking, but he could not understand what she was saying. His mind seemed to be wobbling, losing its balance.

The room was growing dim...dimmer...

Regret...life could have been so different...the son he'd never had...

Silence.

She sat still, watching him until he lost consciousness.

She waited a while longer. Then, to be sure, she pressed an ear to his chest.

When she was certain he was gone, she removed the ropes, tape and gag. Stuffed everything into a plastic bag to take away with her. Then she placed Nash's arms by his sides. Wiped the knife handle and blade, erasing any fingerprints. Pressed the weapon into Nash's hand. Curled the dead fingers around its handle.

She looked down. Spatters of blood on her breasts, arms and legs. There were even spatters on the carpet. Careful not to drip any more onto the carpet, she stepped into the shower and soaped herself all over. Stood under the hot spray for a long time. Then she cleaned the bathroom thoroughly. Dressed.

Placed the suicide note on the bedside table. Grabbed the plastic bag containing the ropes and stuffed it into her handbag. Looked around carefully to make sure she had left nothing. Checked the bathroom once again.

Finally, she took one last look at the man on the bed. He was quite dead.

"Goodbye, George," she said.

She pulled a fashionable black hoodie over her head, opened the door and stepped into the hallway.

Closed the door quietly and left.

Dropped her key in a garbage bin on Thurlow Street.

6

Casey's main duty at the *Clarion* had always been reporting on municipal affairs. Especially as those affairs affected the West End. Inspired by the diaries of Samuel Pepys, he also wrote his "Up and About" column, human-interest pieces.

But things had changed when senior reporter Jack Wexler retired. That was in April, soon after Casey's return from Ireland. Casey now had the crime beat. Always more interested in crime than in city-hall politics, he was more than happy. His first job every weekday morning was what they called cop shop. This meant taking a bus to the Public Safety Building on Main Street for the daily police crime briefings. There was only one downside to this new arrangement. He was still expected to cover the city-hall beat as well.

Casey had tried reasoning with his editor, Percy Simmons.

"Look, Percy, I can't do both jobs properly. It's too much. I'm happy to do cop shop, but you'll need to hire someone to help out with city hall. Then there's the park-board meetings. And all the face-to-faces with council members."

"I'm sorry, Casey, I've no choice," Simmons said. "Debbie's up to her ears in work already. I can't give her more. We can't afford extra staff. It's the way the economy crumbles these days. I could maybe raise your salary a few bucks—"

"I don't care about the money, Perce, you know that."

The editor had laid a hand on Casey's shoulder. "Just do the best you can, Casey, okay? I've asked Debbie to pitch in and help whenever possible. I rely on you two."

Now, Casey waited with other journalists and TV camera operators in a large bare room furnished with a small scatter of folding chairs. Sergeant Joyce Hastings entered the room. She was the communications officer, a tall young woman in police uniform. She sat at a desk in front of a microphone, ready to brief the media.

Casey listened to the usual stuff about robberies, fires and traffic accidents. Then Sergeant Hastings said, "Final item. Shangri-La Hotel staff discovered City Councilor George Hamilton Nash's body in his fortieth-floor condominium early this morning. The councilor's death appeared to be a suicide. Foul play is not suspected. There are no further details. Detective Inspector Plank is in charge of the investigation. That will be all. Good morning, everyone."

Sergeant Hastings got up and left the room.

Casey stared in bewilderment at the empty space left by Hastings. George Nash dead? Suicide? It didn't make sense. Casey had chatted with him at city hall about a month ago. He'd known Nash for—what—five years? Nash had never struck Casey as the suicidal type. He was a rich businessman who enjoyed the good things of life. Food and wine, luxury travel, arts and culture, the company of rich friends. He was the last man in the world to kill himself. Besides, wasn't he planning on running for mayor? If Nash was dead, then it had to be something else. A heart attack or a stroke or something of that sort.

Casey climbed the stairs to DI Plank's office. Plank looked up. "Top o' the morning, Casey. What's up?"

"What's with this Nash suicide stuff, Frank?"

Casey had proved helpful to DI Plank in a recent investigation. Plank had shown his appreciation by allowing Casey easy access to his office. They were friends. Almost.

"Open-and-shut case, buddy," Plank said. "No signs of any monkey business. Of course, the investigation isn't complete until we get the full lab report."

The inspector wore a smart suit and tie. He regarded Casey over the top of his glasses with a friendly grin. He was a heavy man, with sparse gray hair and liquid brown eyes.

Casey said, "I'm not so sure it was suicide, Frank. Could it have been a stroke or a heart attack or—?"

"Off the record, Casey—Nash left a note. Until there's evidence to the contrary, it's suicide."

"Handwritten note? Or typed?"

"Typed. Computer."

"The ME come up with the time of death?"

"Wednesday evening between five and nine, give or take an hour."

"Can I get a crime-scene report?" Casey said.

"I'll fax you a copy. All off the record."

"Of course. Nash used what? Gun, knife?"

"Butcher knife. Cut his arm to the bone, severing the artery. Bed soaked in blood. No signs of a struggle. No signs of the presence of another person. I'm pretty sure the coroner's report will conclude that Nash committed suicide. While the balance of the mind was disturbed, as they say."

"Mind if I see the note?"

"Not available. Crime lab checking it for prints."

"Then maybe I can view the body."

"Right now it's police and coroner's office only. Later maybe."

"Then what about photographs? Could I see—?"

"Look, Casey, it was an ordinary suicide. Man leaves a note, uses sharp blade to sever an artery, bleeds to death. End of story."

"What about motivation? Why did he do it?"

Plank lifted one shoulder. *"Tired of life. Can't take it anymore.* That's what he said in his note."

"What about Nash's wife? Does she say he was tired of life?"

"I still need to see her. They were separated."

"Was the knife found in his hand?" Casey said.

"It was."

"Which one?"

"Which one what?" Plank growled in his raspy voice. He was growing impatient.

"Which hand?"

"Right, of course."

"Why 'of course,' Frank? He could've been left-handed."

Plank sighed. "Not likely. Ninety percent of the population of the planet is right-handed. Close the door behind you, Casey. And leave the police work to us."

Casey got up. "See you later, Frank."

* * *

Brenda handed Casey two typed pages as he came through the door. "Just in," she said.

He nodded his thanks.

Plank's crime-scene report. Casey hung his wet raincoat in the hallway, skimmed the report, then headed into his office. He passed the fax to Debbie Ozeroff at her computer terminal. He waited for her comments.

Debbie looked up in astonishment.

"Councilor Nash? Suicide?"

An attractive woman in her early fifties, Ozeroff had dark hair cut short in the current yellow-streaked fashion. She had a warm, if sometimes excitable, personality. Debbie lived in the West End with Vera Taniguchi, an alternative medicine practitioner.

"*No suspicion of foul play*," Ozeroff read aloud. "Why would a man like George Nash commit suicide? The guy had good looks, and money oozing out of his pores."

"My thought exactly," Casey said.

Ozeroff bent her head to the report. "His Shangri-La condo. Wednesday, between five and nine PM. Makes no sense."

Casey shrugged.

"Who's in charge of the case?" Ozeroff said.

"Detective Inspector Plank."

"Where is our old friend Maggoty these days?"

Maggoty was Ozeroff's disrespectful name for the officious Detective Inspector MacAtee.

"Promoted to superintendent," Casey said.

"Of course. The Peter Principle. The incompetent bungler gets promoted."

Casey said, "Details of Nash's death are off the record. Not much we can print. We wouldn't want to tell our readers the details anyway. Nash bled to death, arm slashed open to the bone."

"Ugh!" Ozeroff said.

Simmons poked his head in the door. "I just heard about Nash," he said.

Ozeroff said, "How long does it take for a man to exsanguinate?"

"To what?" Simmons said.

"Bleed to death," Ozeroff said.

"It'd be quick," Casey said.

"Percy?" Ozeroff said. "You any idea?"

Simmons shook his head. "Depends on the artery. Death could be fast. Could be slow."

Percy Simmons was not only the news editor, managing editor, chief editorial writer and publisher of the *West End Clarion*, he was also the rewrite man and copy editor. A small untidy man in his mid-sixties, he had thick white hair that contrasted with his bushy, expressive dark eyebrows. His wardrobe consisted of outdated clothes. Like today's flared polyester trousers and faded green thrift-shop sweater.

Casey liked Simmons, in spite of—or because of—his old-fashioned ways and opinions. Besides which, he was a darn good editor.

Ozeroff, however, often found their editor tiresome and slow to make decisions. She was also envious of his large, mostly empty office, which he had all to himself. "You ready to talk about trading offices yet, Percy?" she sometimes asked him when she was in a combative mood. "There's three of us in here," she used to say before Jack Wexler retired, "jammed together like goldfish in a pickle jar while skinny little you rattles around that huge office like a bluebottle in a greenhouse. Where's your sense of fairness? Where's your sense of common dec—?"

Simmons always ignored Ozeroff's complaints, rolling his eyes to the ceiling and emitting a long-suffering sigh.

Now, he looked down at his ancient Hush Puppies and shook his head. "Maybe you could do an obituary on him, Casey, okay?"

Casey nodded. "I'll get on it, Percy."

7

When Sunday came around again, he had his whiskey and soda ready. The telephone rang. He picked up the receiver and listened to her voice with pleasure. Her accent was rediscovering its Irish lilt. She was tired.

It had been a long day. Her mother was comfortable. She had mixed smoothies for them both, but her mother could take very little. She read aloud to her mother for short periods. Mostly, though, the old woman slept.

He told her about cop shop. How much he enjoyed it. How he and Ozeroff missed Jack Wexler now that he had retired. How much he missed her. How much he was looking forward to her returning home. Ireland was no longer her home. She belonged in Vancouver now, with him. How much he loved her.

When they were done talking, he bade her goodnight, even though it was only two o'clock in Vancouver. Then he fixed himself another whiskey and soda.

Neither of them had mentioned John Burns.

* * *

Back from cop shop on Monday morning, Casey carried two coffees into the office and handed one to Ozeroff.

"Thanks, Casey. You're a lifesaver. Anything new on the Nash suicide?"

"Nothing," Casey said.

"You find out anything on Nash's wife?" Ozeroff said.

"Not much. Her name is Moira. Otherwise, the information is about the same as before. Husband George walked out on her. More than twenty years of marriage and he walks out. Leaves his fancy penthouse on Stanley Park and moves into an even fancier new condo in the Shangri-La. He's alone. No other woman in the picture, far as I know."

"Walked out on his wife and offed himself a couple months later," Ozeroff said.

Casey nodded. "That's about it, Deb."

"Who owns the Shangri-La condo?"

"Nash."

"Two luxury condos," Ozeroff said. "Won't need them now."

"Multimillionaire," Casey said. "One of the richest men in the city." He sat in his swivel chair and rocked gently. "He was," he added. He stared out through their rain-streaked office windows at a moving blur of pedestrians and umbrellas on Denman Street.

"Any kids?"

"No kids."

"You really think he committed suicide?"

"No."

"Then it was homicide."

"Most likely."

"Who stands to gain from his death?" Ozeroff said.

Casey shrugged. "Probably his wife." He checked his watch. "I better take care of Nash's obituary. Got a face-to-face lined up with his wife."

"You need me along?" Ozeroff said.

"I do," Casey said. "Thanks, Deb."

* * *

Moira Nash buzzed them into the Roosevelt Building. They took an elevator up to the penthouse. A small woman in nurse's uniform opened the door and let them in. Mrs. Nash, standing with the aid of a cane, was waiting for them in the living room.

"I'm Casey of the *Clarion*, and this is my colleague, Debbie Ozeroff."

"Thank you, Gerda," Mrs. Nash said to the nurse. Turning to her guests, she said, "Please sit down."

The nurse melted away.

The apartment was huge. Casey and Ozeroff sat at opposite ends of a large beige sofa. Moira Nash sat facing them, on an upholstered wing chair. Posture straight and formal. Casey tried to study her without staring. Fine-looking woman. Short dark hair to the neck, blond highlights, milk-pale skin, gray eyes. She wore a simple blue dress fitted to her slender figure. Shoes to match. Except for the cane in her hand, she could have been posing for *Vogue* magazine.

"We're sorry for your loss, Mrs. Nash," Casey said.

"Please call me Moira."

"The *Clarion* is running an obituary on Councilor Nash," Casey said. "We'd like your input."

Moira nodded. "Of course," she said quietly. "I have already made some notes for you. I think you will find them helpful." She passed him an envelope.

"Your husband was an important man," Casey said, weighing the envelope in his hand.

She bowed her head. Then she looked up. "My husband and I are separated. Since April. After twenty-one years of marriage."

Casey and Ozeroff remained silent.

"He was a disappointment," Moira continued. "You would perhaps understand my feelings if you were abandoned suddenly, without notice, only a week away from major surgery."

"Surgery?" Ozeroff said. "Then we shouldn't disturb you further." She stood.

Casey stood also. "We'll go, Mrs. Nash—Moira," he said.

"Please sit down," Moira said.

They sat.

"The surgery was a month ago. My husband was cruel. There. Now you have it. You can print that in your obituary if you like. 'George Hamilton Nash was a cruel man!' I said so to the police when they were here."

Moira spoke softly. Ironically, her quiet tone lent more power to the harsh words.

Casey looked uneasily at Ozeroff, who looked uneasily back at Casey.

"You know we can't print that, Moira," Ozeroff said. "But you have our sympathy. We wish you a swift recovery."

Silence.

"It was a hip replacement," Moira said. "Recovery depends on intimate help at home. I was forced to hire a stranger, a nurse."

"You appear to be recovering well," Ozeroff said.

"Yes," Moira said, "with the help of a good nurse. Gerda has been a lifesaver."

Silence.

"Your husband's death must have come as a great shock to you," Casey said.

"Yes," she said.

Silence.

"Mrs. Nash—Moira," Casey said, "do you know of any reason why your husband might have taken his life?"

Moira shook her head. "None, Mr. Casey."

"It's just Casey," Casey said.

"Was he depressed?" Ozeroff said.

"Just the opposite," Moira said quietly. "He was looking forward to living alone. Away from me."

"Mr. Nash left a note," Casey said. *"I can't live with myself.* His exact words."

"That doesn't sound like George," Moira said.

"What about Mr. Nash's business?" Casey said. "Any problems there, do you know?"

Again she shook her head. "None that I know of. But he had many business interests. I have included the names and telephone numbers of two business partners in my notes."

"Do you have children?" Ozeroff said.

"None," Moira said.

Casey said, "Did Mr. Nash leave you— pardon the question, for it has nothing to do with the obituary—did he leave you for... someone else? I know it's none of our business, but as an investigative reporter, I always like—" He stopped, leaving his sentence hanging.

Moira was silent for a moment. Then she spoke. "You're right, Casey. It isn't any of your business. But I'm not proud. George, to my knowledge, had always been a faithful husband." She frowned and regarded her fingernails, as if mentally rehearsing what to say. Then she said, "For about a year or so, before George left, a woman called here several times a month, asking to speak to my husband. A woman. She told me her name but..." Moira shrugged. "I can't remember it.

It's just council business, George assured me. I believed him, of course. At the time."

"But now you don't?" Ozeroff said.

"No," Moira said. "He left me because he wanted to live alone. That's what he said. But now I'm convinced he was having an affair— or had a mistress. I shouldn't be telling you all this." Tears sprang to her eyes. "But I've no one else to tell." Her eyes widened. "Nothing of this will appear in your paper, I hope."

"Not a word," Casey said. "But if you think of the caller's name—the woman—could you let us know?"

She nodded.

"Do you believe Mr. Nash committed suicide?" Casey said.

Moira dried her eyes on a tiny handkerchief. "I don't know. My mind is so confused, I don't seem to know anything for sure."

"You have been most helpful," Casey said as they got up to leave.

"Thanks for meeting with us," Ozeroff said.

Mrs. Nash stood. She tapped her cane on the floor. The nurse came and showed them to the door.

"Oh, Moira, there's just one more question," Casey said as they were leaving. "Was Mr. Nash right- or left-handed?"

"Left," Moira said.

The nurse closed the door.

* * *

"So what do you think, Deb? Was it murder or was it suicide?"

"I've no idea."

They were walking back to the office in the drizzling rain. Ozeroff had her umbrella. Casey wore his trusty cap.

Casey said, "If it was suicide, then why was the knife found in the right hand of a left-handed man? Wouldn't a left-handed man be more likely to slash his right arm?"

"Good point," Ozeroff said.

"And where's the motive?" Casey said. "Nash was, as far as anyone knows, a healthy man with a bright future. If it was murder, did Moira Nash kill her husband? No children. She stands to inherit a great deal of money."

"She'd be my main suspect," Ozeroff said. "Underneath her confusion Moira is angry,

I think. She fought hard to control it. But I sensed it, under the surface. I'd be angry too if my husband walked out on me. Maybe she hired a hit man."

"Or hit woman. Thanks for coming with me, Deb."

"Don't mention it, Casey," Ozeroff said.

8

Moira Nash called Casey the next day.

"The woman who telephoned so often. I heard George call her Cally."

"How's it spelled?"

"I have no idea."

"Thanks, Mrs. Nash. I'll be in touch if I learn anything."

* * *

"Do me a favor, Deb?"

"Sure, Casey. You want me to leave Vera and run away with you?"

"Not yet, Deb. I'll let you know when I'm ready. Meanwhile, I want you to use your superior research skills to find all the information you can on Nash's business partners. The first is Joanne Drummond of Oasis Investments."

"Like what?"

"Reputation of her company, her boyfriends, lifestyle, including recent changes in her life, where she lives, what she pays in rent, what she eats for breakfast, brand of toothpaste she uses—the works. The same background check on Nash's second partner, Sam Spencer of Everest Enterprises."

"Will I be able to get a reference from you if I apply for a job with the FBI?"

"Of course."

* * *

After cop shop on Wednesday morning, Casey took a bus ride to the Harding Building downtown.

Nash's second partner, Sam Spencer, occupied a luxurious office at Everest Enterprises on the seventeenth floor of the building. He was a small balding man. It was difficult for Casey to guess his age. Could have been anything from forty to sixty. His name appeared in gold leaf on his office door. He wore horn-rimmed glasses and an expensive dark business suit with a colorful silk tie.

Standing up from behind a neat mahogany desk, Spencer offered his hand. "You must be Sebastian Casey of the *Clarion*."

"It's just Casey," Casey said. "Just want to ask a few questions about your friend and partner George Nash. About his untimely death."

"Of course. Please sit down, Casey."

Casey took a seat.

Spencer sat behind his desk. "I'm glad you're here. The fact is, I have questions of my own about George's death. I was with him a few days before he died and…" He paused.

"Yes, go on."

"We lunched together, at the Vancouver Hotel, just the two of us."

Spencer became agitated, rising from behind his desk and slowly pacing the carpeted floor.

"How did he seem to you? I mean, was he in good spirits?" Casey asked, swiveling his chair to follow Spencer's movements.

"Excellent spirits," Spencer said. "We'd just concluded a very profitable piece of business that morning. So we celebrated with wine over lunch. The last I saw of him he was on Burrard Street, waving back at me. A big cheerful grin on his face. A few days later he was dead. And the police were calling it suicide. I don't understand it."

He sat down heavily in his office chair, shaking his head.

"George wasn't the suicidal type, whatever type that is. But he had no reason to kill himself. George was one of the most level-headed guys I know. I called the police to tell them they were crazy. They eventually put me through to an Inspector Plank, who said he'd be dropping by to see me."

"Did Nash say anything about his future plans?"

"Nothing special that I can think of."

"And business is good. No problems of any kind."

"None."

"Thanks, Mr. Spencer. I'm sorry you lost your friend. Please call me if you hear anything further. For what it's worth, I don't think Nash killed himself either."

"You think he was murd—?"

"I don't know, Mr. Spencer, but I would sure like to find out."

* * *

Casey ate a quick Subway sandwich on Robson Street, then set out for the Public Safety Building and went looking for DI Plank.

He was in his office, shuffling papers.

Casey sat himself down. "Afternoon, Frank."

"I'm busy, Casey. Unless you got something for me."

"Maybe I have."

"Like what?"

"You first. I'd like to see that suicide note."

Plank picked up a file from his desk and handed him a piece of paper. A photocopy of the note, undated and unsigned. Casey read the note, written all in capitals.

I CAN'T LIVE WITH MYSELF ANY
   LONGER
LIFE IS TOO TEDIOUS AND GRIM
I'M SORRY MOYRA

He handed it back.

"Look, Frank, I'm convinced Nash didn't kill himself."

"Oh yeah?"

"I think he was murdered," Casey said.

"Murdered. You gotta be kiddin' me," Plank said. "I've told you before—"

"Hear me out. First, there's his state of mind. Everyone, including his wife and one of his business partners, says he was a guy too fond of life to kill himself. I talked to Nash myself in his office at city hall. Told me about his plans to run for mayor. He had ambitions, Frank. Second, according to Nash's wife, he was left-handed. He was found, you say, with a knife in his right hand. Third, that note you just showed me is phony. It's unlikely Nash would misspell his wife's name."

"How does the wife spell her name?"

"*M-O-I-R-A*," said Casey, spelling it out for him.

"Son of a bitch," Plank said.

"See you later, Inspector."

9

Following cop shop on Thursday morning, Casey had a face-to-face at city hall with his friend Councilor Ross Brierley.

Brierley smiled in welcome. They shook hands. "Take a seat, Casey," he said. "What can I do for you, pal?"

An experienced councilor, Brierley was in his late forties. Blond and handsome with chiseled features, he looked good in a dark pinstripe suit, pink shirt, red and blue tie and black wingtips.

Casey asked him about Councilor George Hamilton Nash.

"Was he well liked on council?" Casey said.

"So-so. Good points and bad. Good head. A bit pompous."

"You know of anyone might want to kill him?"

Brierley shook his head. "Nobody. I thought the police said it was a suicide."

"Yeah, but I'm not so sure," Casey said. "Would you happen to know if he was having an affair? Gay or straight."

Brierley laughed. "You don't fool me, Casey," he said. "I'm well aware of your reputation as an amateur detective. You're hoping Gorgeous George was murdered and you can collar his killer, am I right?"

Casey smiled modestly.

"My opinion? I don't know if he was having an affair. But Nash was straight as they come. Never met a woman he didn't like."

"You know of any particular woman or women he hit on here at city hall?"

"Friendly with them all," Brierley said. "Wouldn't be surprised, though, if he had something going with that new secretary of his. Young and fresh. She wasn't out of the city-hall secretarial pool. Hired her himself."

"Know her name?" Casey said.

"Pauline something. Lost her job when poor old George popped his clogs. Not in the pool, you see."

"Could you get her name and address for me?"

"Privileged information, I'm afraid."

"Naturally."

Brierley grinned. "I'll see what I can do for you, Casey. Check back with me before you leave the building."

"Also," Casey said, "do you know anyone named Cally works in the building?"

"Cally?" Brierley thought for a moment. "No," he said. "Can't help you there, pal."

"Thanks, Ross. Appreciate your help."

* * *

Casey made his way down to the busy coffee shop in the basement. Found a seat at the counter. He looked about him, recognizing many of the faces. Regular staff members, most of them. He was just about to join a reporter from *The Province* when he spotted the council secretary, Margaret Mullen, coming through the door.

"Can I buy you a coffee, Ms. Mullen? I'm Casey of the *Clarion*."

"Thanks." She smiled and sat beside him at the counter. "I know who you are, Casey of the *Clarion*. I've noticed you dozing in the media benches. I'll have a green tea."

Casey ordered.

Mullen was attractive, with a trim figure and short dark hair to the shoulders. A jean skirt covered her knees. A black silk shirt with a high collar. High black boots. Minimal makeup. She looked about thirty but could be thirty-five, Casey guessed. Faint perfume fresh, like freesias. No wedding ring.

He thought of Emma. It would be about six in the evening in Ireland right now. Was John Burns taking her out for a drink at the local pub? Was he sweet-talking her? Holding her hand? Telling her stories about the famous writers he knew?

Mullen was talking. Casey thrust Emma from his thoughts.

"I try to read all your 'Up and About' pieces," Mullen was saying. "I like your sense of humor."

He nodded.

"But with that broken nose, you look more like a tough guy than a funny man," she said.

"Not broken, Ms. Mullen, just slightly bent."

"Please call me Maggie." She looked into his eyes. "We have something in common, it seems."

"We do?"

"Irish names," she said. "I took my mother's name, Mullen. She was born in County Wicklow, not far from Glendalough."

"What happened to your father?"

She closed her eyes and shook her head. "He left us. I was only a kid. Four years old. My mother never talked about him except to say he went off with another woman. She changed her name back to what it was before she married him. Changed my name too. Didn't want his name in our lives."

Casey nodded. "Was your father Irish too?"

"No. He was from there, but I don't want to talk about him. He's dead, as far as I'm concerned."

He liked her. Soft voice. Friendly personality.

"I plan to visit Ireland someday. Sooner rather than later, I hope," she said.

Her eyes were blue. Darker than Emma's. Bolder too.

"You didn't invite me to join you just so you could charm me with your winning Irish ways, am I right?" Maggie said. "You either want insider news for the *Clarion* or you'd like to ask me out for a drink some evening. Possibly both."

"You saw into my black heart," Casey said.

They looked into each other's eyes for several beats as they sipped their drinks.

Then Casey said, "You ever have much to do with Councilor George Nash?"

Maggie shook her head. "Not really. We'd say good morning, that's about it."

"What did you think of him?"

She shrugged. "Seemed like a nice enough guy."

"You ever see or hear him argue or get mad at anyone?"

"No."

"You ever notice him being extra friendly with any of the women at city hall?"

"Nope. Why so interested in Nash? The poor dope committed suicide, right?"

"The police think so. But I wonder why a man with so much going for him would decide to end his life."

"No one can ever know another person's heart, my mother says." She frowned. "But why the curiosity? Do you think he was murdered?"

"Maybe."

"Then why not leave the questions for the police to answer?"

Casey shrugged. "I'm an investigative reporter."

"You must tell me more some other time. But right now I've got to get back," Maggie said.

"Just one more question. You ever hear of a woman works here name of Cally?"

"Cally? No. Don't think so."

Casey stood, left a bill on the counter and walked Maggie to the elevator.

"Nice talking to you, Casey. Maybe you can ask me out for that drink sometime."

"Don't see why not."

Before leaving the building, he checked back with Ross Brierley. Ross had the goods for him. George Hamilton Nash's former secretary was Pauline Parker, a West Ender. Lived in a rented apartment on Broughton Street.

* * *

Pauline Parker was expecting him but wouldn't take the chain off her door until she had seen some ID.

He passed a business card through the gap in the door.

"Wait there one minute, okay?"

He could hear her making a call to the *Clarion* office.

A minute later she took the chain off and opened the door.

"Brenda described you very well," Parker said. "Big guy with red hair, bent nose and Irish accent. That's you, all right. I just made a fresh pot of coffee. Would you like some, Sebastian?"

"It's Casey," Casey said.

Brierley was right. She was young and fresh. Handpicked by the lately departed Councilor Nash, she was probably in her mid-twenties. Tall and slim, dark hair in a ponytail. Graceful like a dancer. She wore black tights, a long plain yellow T-shirt to her thighs and well-worn leather moccasins.

There was very little furniture in the apartment. Two packing cases did the work of tables. Casey sat in the only decent chair, a well-worn specimen from the 1950s. She pulled up a packing crate, placed his coffee on it and then sat on the rug facing him, legs folded under her, back straight.

"You know they laid me off, don't you?" Parker said.

English accent. Sounded like the queen.

Casey nodded.

"Arseholes," Parker said. English pronunciation.

Casey nodded again.

"What do you want, Casey?"

"Just a couple questions about your former boss."

"Fire away."

Casey seldom made notes in face-to-faces. The sight of a pen and notebook scared most people off. "Did you like your boss, Councilor Nash?"

Parker shrugged. "He was all right."

"Did you have a relationship with him?"

She giggled. "Sleep with him, you mean?"

Casey nodded.

"Will anything I say be printed in your paper?"

"Not a word."

"That a promise?"

"A promise," Casey said.

"We only shagged a few months—make that four." She grinned. "He thought he was God's gift to women."

"Where did you meet to do this, er—?"

"Shagging? His apartment, of course."

"Which was where?"

"Tallest building in the city. Shangri-La. Big fancy place on the fortieth floor, which is actually only the thirty-ninth because they don't have a thirteenth. What kind of medieval thinking is that? View of sea and mountains. What a pad! I thought I'd finally made it."

"Did you tell all this to the police?" Casey said.

"Police? I haven't seen the police. The papers said it was a suicide."

"I'm not so sure," Casey said.

Parker's eyes widened. "You think he was murdered?"

"Possibly. Did you kill him, Parker?"

"No way!" she said, happily bouncing her shapely behind on her heels. "I'm the kind of girl who wouldn't hurt an earwig. How did he die? Was he shot?"

"Do you know anyone who might've killed him?"

"Not a clue."

"You ever see or hear him arguing or fighting with anyone?"

"Never."

"You ever hear of anyone working at city hall by the name of Cally?"

"Cally? Nope."

"What kind of work did you do in England, Parker? Secretarial, same as here?"

"I was a registered nurse. In the OR, Cheltenham General Hospital."

"OR?" Casey said.

"Operating room. Surgical procedures. I'll go back to it eventually. But I needed a break. It's quite intensive work. I needed a rest."

"You would see a lot of blood in that job, I'm sure," Casey said.

"Yes, you could say that." She laughed. "But one gets used to it."

Casey stood. "Thanks for the coffee, Parker."

"My pleasure," Parker said, rising fluidly from her position on the rug. Like a time-lapse film of a burgeoning sunflower. "In the meantime, if you hear of a job in the newspaper business, you let me know, okay? Drop in for coffee anytime. Bring some cake or biscuits if you can."

10

Friday cop shop.

Sergeant Joyce Hastings in charge. Starting with the small stuff and working up to the large. "Last item," she said. "City Councilor George Nash's death last week is now being treated as a homicide."

There were questions. "Why the change from suicide?" someone asked.

"New evidence in the case," Hastings said. "That will be all. Good morning, everyone."

Casey rushed off, but Plank wasn't in his office. He found him in the cafeteria.

"Hey, what's new, Frank?"

"We can talk in my office."

Casey followed him back.

Plank sat down and sighed. "This is off the record, remember. Turns out the corpse had wrist and ankle abrasions. Nash was tied, or handcuffed, to the bed. Also, some skin abrasion of lips and mouth. Duct-tape damage."

"The victim was bound to the bed and gagged while someone slashed his artery open."

Plank nodded.

"Meaning you missed the abrasions first time round, right?"

Plank growled, "They didn't show up until the body had been lying twenty-four hours in the morgue. Nash bled to death, remember? I warned you before, Casey. Leave the police work to the professionals."

Casey made for the door. "Thanks for the update, Inspector."

* * *

He returned to the newspaper office with two Starbucks coffees.

"Thanks, Casey," Ozeroff said. "You're a mind reader."

Simmons poked his head around the door. "Coffee time?"

"Didn't get you one. Sorry, Perce."

Simmons shrugged. "Any exciting news from cop shop?"

"Nash's death is now a homicide," Casey said. "It's official. Marks made by wrist and ankle restraints showed up at the morgue."

"Can we print any of this?" Simmons said.

Casey shook his head. "Off the record, Perce."

"Ropes and handcuffs?" Ozeroff said. "Playing sex games. Then the killer's obviously a woman."

"Could be a man," Casey said.

"I guess so," Ozeroff said. "She—or he—tied Nash to the bed. Helpless lamb to the slaughter. Enjoyed watching him die, probably. Revenge maybe. Bleeding to death. Lots of time for him to think." She paused. "And to suffer."

"That's some sick imagination you got there, Debbie," Simmons said.

Ozeroff grinned up at him. "I know. Don't ya love it?"

* * *

Sunday, and no call from Emma.

* * *

On Monday, Casey was in the office of Joanne Drummond, Nash's other business partner.

He was there to ask her a few questions. But his mind kept skipping to an image of Emma and John Burns together. What had prevented her from calling this time?

Drummond was waiting for him to speak.

"How long had you known George Nash?" Casey asked.

"Over twenty years," Drummond said. "We met as students at UBC. I see in the papers they're calling it a homicide now."

Drummond wore a smart gray business suit—jacket and slacks. Needed to lose ten or fifteen pounds to be fashionably slim. Right now her pleasantly open face was lined with concern.

"You ever have any serious disagreements or arguments?" Casey said.

"Arguments with George? Never." She laughed. "He was much too easygoing."

"I understand that you run Oasis Investments on your own, is that right? That George was a silent partner?"

Drummond nodded. "He left management to me. But I'll miss him an awful lot. I knew he was always there if I needed him."

"You bought a new BMW sports car recently."

"Huh?"

"Paid in cash."

Drummond frowned. "I don't see what—"

"You also bought a house in Kitsilano."

She stared at him, openmouthed. "That's none of your fuckin' business."

"And a cottage on—"

Joanne Drummond sprang to her feet and held her office door open.

"This interview is over, Mr. Casey. Goodbye."

11

The first things Casey noticed when he inspected the carpeted lobby and hallways of the sixty-two-story Shangri-La Hotel were the discreet state-of-the-art security cameras.

The security office was in the basement of the hotel, at the end of a long uncarpeted and deserted corridor. Casey knocked on the door. When there was no response, he pushed the door open. The office was empty except for a desk and a chair. A gray uniform cap sat on the desk.

A gray security uniform jacket hung on the back of the chair. Behind the desk was a closed door. Casey could hear groaning sounds coming from behind the door. He opened the door and found the security guard pushing a woman hard up against the wall, his trousers down around his ankles, the woman's skirt up around her hips.

"Excuse me," Casey said.

He turned and left. He waited outside in the corridor for a count of ten and then, after knocking, re-entered the office.

The woman, a no-longer-young blond, rushed by him on her way out the door.

He introduced himself to the security guard, now behind his desk, putting on his uniform jacket.

The guard's name, Anthony Donizetti, appeared on his lapel pin.

"Homicide in suite four-zero-zero-four, May twenty-third. I would like to see the security-camera tape for that evening," Casey said.

"The police have already inspected that tape, Mr. Casey, and I'm afraid it's no longer—"

"It's just Casey. Sorry for busting in on you just now, Anthony."

They stared at one another for a couple of beats.

Casey smiled.

Donizetti leaped to his feet. "No problem, Casey. Let me get that tape for you. The period of time examined by the police is marked. It'll be easy to locate. Please follow me."

He led Casey into the passion room, loaded the tape into a VCR and fast-forwarded it to 6:12 PM. Then he switched off the main light, leaving Casey alone in front of the monitor.

Casey moved the black-and-white tape forward, watching pictures of the deserted hallway outside Nash's door. It didn't take long for the figure of a woman to come into view, at 6:15 PM. The angle of the camera was high. The woman, if it was a woman, carried a handbag and wore a hoodie that obscured her face. She inserted a key in the lock and let herself in. All of which took only seconds.

Then not long after, at 6:30 PM, Nash appeared and let himself in. The door closed once again.

Casey moved the tape forward. At 7:25 PM, the door opened and the woman came out of the apartment, still wearing her hoodie and carrying her handbag. She did not look up. She did not lock the door. It was obvious to Casey that the woman knew of the security camera· and had worn the hoodie to make it impossible to identify her.

He looked at the complete sequence one more time, stopping the tape on the woman for careful examination. He saw nothing that might help ID her. She was just an average, ordinary woman in a hoodie. For that matter, it could even be a man in disguise.

He had drawn a blank.

"Thanks, Anthony," Casey said, leaving. "Have a good day now."

* * *

Sunday at two.

Whiskey and soda.

"Ma's gone, Casey." Emma cried into the telephone. "Passed away in the small hours before dawn. I heard her call out. I went to her and held her hands. I felt her leaving me. It was physical. Like she wanted me there to see her go. Waited for me to say goodbye.

75

But not a word she spoke. But rose up out of the house she'd lived in all her life and left it behind her. Her leaving was the quietest thing. Like a sparrow flying up the chimney and into the sky."

"I'm sorry for your trouble, Emma."

"Oh, Casey!"

"She's resting now, in peace."

"She is. I'll finish up here. There's a lot to do—the house needs to be sold. A couple of weeks and then I'll be home, I'm hoping. I miss Vancouver. But mostly I miss you, Casey. I even miss the awful Vancouver rain. It rained here this morning, but it's not the same. It's…"

"Soft," they said together, laughing.

"I will call next Sunday," Emma said. "I love you, Casey."

"I'm waiting for you, girl."

12

Ross Brierley stood up from behind his desk, hand extended.

"I need a huge favor, Ross," Casey said, shaking his hand. "You remember last time

I was here? I was asking about a city hall employee named Cally? Well, I've got to find her. That means a search in the employee data bank for someone I can pin that nickname on."

"Restricted information, Casey. Sorry."

"It could lead to George Nash's killer."

Brierley shook his sleek head.

Casey said, "You could connect with the data bank and accidentally leave it on. Then you could take a break in the coffee shop while I—"

"But there are hundreds of employees on that list. It would take an hour or more. I can't leave you in here with—"

"Take a lunch hour, Ross. On me. I promise I won't tamper with the list."

"You couldn't without the password, and even I don't have that."

Brierley logged in to the data bank and then gave Casey his seat. "I'll give you half an hour, Casey. Not a minute more. That's the best I can do."

He left his office, closing the door behind him.

* * *

Less than an hour later Casey was back at the *Clarion* office, talking with Ozeroff.

"You remember the name Moira Nash gave me?" Casey said. "Cally?"

"Moira said the woman called Nash at home a lot."

"That's the one. I tracked her down."

"She works at city hall?"

"You got it. I think it is probably Angela Brill. She's a councilor. Her middle name is Calista."

"Cally for short," Ozeroff said. "I bet she'll turn out to be Nash's mistress."

Casey punched ten digits into his desk phone.

"Could I get an appointment with Councilor Brill?" he said.

"What name, please?"

"Casey, *West End Clarion*."

"One moment, please."

Casey chewed the end of his pencil.

He waited.

"Mr. Casey?"

"Yes?"

"There's no need for an appointment. Ms. Brill is here Mondays and Fridays, in the afternoon. She's usually available. Come to the council offices anytime before four."

Casey made for the door. "See you later, Deb. I'm off for a face-to-face with Councilor Angela Cally Brill herself."

* * *

Casey could see Brill sitting behind a desk in the empty council chamber. He tried the glass door, but it was locked. He rapped his knuckles on the glass. As she got up to let him in, he watched her swift, confident stride and swirling skirt.

Casey's usual view of Councilor Brill was from behind his media desk. From there, she appeared to be attractive. But close up, Angela Brill wasn't merely attractive—she was beautiful. Classic features, straight, fine blond hair to below the shoulders. Hazel eyes and a peaches-and-cream complexion. All packaged alluringly in a gray skirt, white shirt and black heels. Tiny invisible motes of expensive perfume circled about her.

"Come in and take a seat," she said, smiling at Casey and indicating the city clerk's empty chair.

He sat. Her ring finger was bare, he noticed.

She occupied the council secretary's seat, moving her chair so she could look him in the eye.

"Thanks for seeing me," Casey said.

Luminous smile. "It's a pleasure. I always read your 'Up and About' pieces in the *Clarion*, Sebastian—may I call you that?"

"Everyone calls me Casey. You, too, are entertaining. I watch and listen to you at council meetings. I enjoyed your remarks on the topic of homeless chickens. I also admired your research on the Olympic Village financial fiasco. And your speech about the rights of the Falun Gong people to continue their protest in their little shack outside the Chinese embassy. It was spot-on, I thought."

"Thank you, Casey." Brill leaned back in her chair, fingertips together, eyebrows raised, waiting for him to start.

She was a cool customer, he could see that. Perfect control. He wasn't about to win her with flattery.

"So, Casey?" she said after a while. She crinkled her eyes at him in a friendly manner.

"George Hamilton Nash," Casey said. "I'm investigating his recent death. I wonder if you can—"

"But isn't that the job of the police?"

"It is. But the police need all the help they can get, don't you think? Investigative journalism can sometimes play a small part in helping bring criminals to justice."

Her luminous smile had disappeared. "Criminals? But Councilor Nash committed suicide."

"You haven't heard? The police have upped it a notch. To homicide."

She said nothing, but for a brief instant something happened in her eyes. Casey caught a sense of her pulling back, losing a thin slice of that perfect control.

"You must have seen quite a lot of Councilor Nash," Casey said.

"I beg your pardon?"

"Sorry. Clumsy of me. I meant you must have seen him many times. At council meetings here in this chamber, and in and around

81

the offices. Two councilors working together, so to speak."

"Of course."

"Did you ever see Councilor Nash at other times?" Casey said.

"I don't know what you're suggesting, but the answer is no. We were, however, good friends. We often discussed council matters together over coffee or lunch."

"Do you know, Ms. Brill, if Nash was well liked by the other council members and city-hall staff? Did he have any enemies, to your knowledge?"

"None as far as I know," Brill said.

"That's all?" Casey said.

"What do you mean?" Brill said, frowning.

"Can you think of anyone who would want him dead?"

"No."

"Did you ever call Councilor Brill at his home?"

"I can't recall…"

"Using the name Cally?"

Brill blushed. "It's short for Calista, my middle name. Friends call me Cally.

I occasionally called him at home, yes. But only if there was something important on my mind regarding council business."

"You had no relationship outside of council business?" Casey said.

"Not at all. Councilor Nash was a married man."

"Do you remember what you were doing on the evening of May twenty-third?"

"Is that when he died? You're asking if I have an alibi? Well, no, I don't. I was probably at home, writing as usual. Either that or I was washing and ironing. I don't remember."

"Writing?"

"Yes. I write books for young people."

"Children?"

"Precisely."

"Do you have children of your own?"

"None. I'm not married."

"Thanks, Ms. Brill. You have been helpful. If you think of anything, please give me a call." He left his card on her desk. "I'll find my way out."

He hadn't learned much about George Nash's death.

But he had learned a little about Ms. Angela Calista Brill, also known as Cally.

* * *

Casey got back to the office as Ozeroff was about to leave for the day.

"What is she like, this Cally Brill lady?" Ozeroff said. "She look like a murderer?"

"Not a bit. She's a good-looker and she's smart. Also, she's really..." He thought for a moment. "She's really very nice."

"Then she's a murderer for sure," Ozeroff said.

13

The next day at Hegel's Bagels on Denman Street, Casey, Ozeroff and Simmons occupied a table near the window.

Casey looked out at the late-spring sunshine and the huge splashes of color in Morton Park. Rhododendrons, flowering dogwoods, azaleas. Laughing bronze giants. Beyond the borders full of colorful flowers lay English Bay's sandy beach and glittering green ocean. Beyond the ocean, white-topped mountains reached up to a clear blue sky. Vancouver at its best.

Their editor almost never lunched with them. But today there was much to discuss. Simmons had wanted a meeting in his office, but a hungry Ozeroff insisted he come along with them to Hegel's. He could have his meeting there, she told him. "It will do you good, Percy, to see how your serfs are forced to subsist on the cheapest and most basic of foods."

Now the only topic left to discuss was the Nash murder.

"So anything new?" Simmons asked Casey.

"The killer could be Councilor Angela Brill," Casey said quietly. "Or it could be Nash's partner Joanne Drummond."

"You have any evidence?" Simmons said.

"Joanne Drummond definitely had a motive. I think Nash discovered she was cheating their clients. Maybe even running a Ponzi scheme. He probably threatened to go to the police. So she shut him up with the help of a butcher knife."

"What about Brill?" Simmons said.

"Many calls to Nash at home," Casey said. "Could've been his mistress. I'm pretty sure he had a mistress at city hall. Brill might be a good candidate. Then he started sleeping with Pauline Parker, his new secretary. I think Brill or somebody found out. And had her revenge by killing him. I haven't a shred of proof for any of this, of course."

"Theories are not evidence," Simmons said. "What do the police think?"

"I've no idea what the police think," Casey said.

Simmons said, "Look, Casey, it's our job to report the news, not make it. I don't want you wasting any more time on George Nash." He stood. "I'm out of here. Leave police work to the police, okay?"

Where had he heard that before?

Simmons left.

"Your theories about those two women," Ozeroff said. "They would have to be mental cases for sure."

"For sure," Casey said.

* * *

"Just dropped in to give you a heads up, Frank."

DI Plank looked up from his desk. "Big of you, Casey. Like what?"

"Couple of things on the Nash case. His business partner, Joanne Drummond. She's been spending a lot of money this past year or so."

"We're already on to her, Casey. New home, BMW, holiday cottage. A forensic audit is under way off the record, by the way."

"You think she's the one?"

"Too soon to say."

"Okay, then get this," Casey said. "Councilor Angela Brill's middle name is Calista, Cally for short. According to Moira, Nash's wife, a city-hall woman by the name of Cally often called George Nash at his home. Good-looking woman. Looks to me like Brill could be Nash's mistress. But then Nash started bonking his new secretary. A young cutie named Pauline Parker. Brill found out. In a jealous rage Brill killed Nash and tried to make it look like a suicide."

"Makes a good story, but it's all circumstantial," Plank said. "Have you got one solid piece of evidence?"

"Not really."

Plank sighed. "Casey, why don't you just leave the—"

"Yes, I know, Frank. Leave the police work to the police."

* * *

The next afternoon Casey found himself close to Broughton Street. He decided to call Pauline Parker, George Nash's former secretary.

"I'd like to drop by, if that's okay."

"Casey! How lovely. I could use a little cheering up. More questions?"

"A couple."

"How soon can you be here?"

"See you in fifteen."

"Perfect. Gives me time to make fresh coffee."

He buzzed her apartment and she let him in.

He handed her a bag. "I picked up some cookies—biscuits."

"Most thoughtful of you. Thanks, Casey." She looked in the bag. "Arrowroots! Lovely."

He made himself comfortable in the same chair as before.

Parker brought the coffee and biscuits. They sipped and crunched quietly.

Today she was wearing a tracksuit, which covered up her curves, and nothing on her pale and elegant feet.

"You ever have anything much to do with Councilor Angela Brill when you were working for Nash?"

Parker smiled. "Councilor Brill? That's the glamorous blond. She was around quite a bit— in and out of Nash's office—but she never said anything to me. Seemed okay."

"When she went into his office, did they close the door?"

"I don't think so. Usually it was ajar. I could listen to them if I wanted."

"Did you listen?" Casey said.

"Sometimes. But they were just yakking about boring council stuff."

"Are you sure? Is there a possibility they were having an affair?"

Parker shrugged and reached for an arrowroot. "Looked perfectly proper to me."

"You're sure?"

"Sure I'm sure."

They sat in silence for a while, Casey digesting what Parker had said.

Then Parker said, "That's it? No more questions?"

"No more questions."

"You think someone at city hall is the murderer, right?"

"It's possible," Casey said. "How's the job hunt going?"

Parker pulled a face. "There're only service jobs out there. Minimum wage. I think I might go back to the UK. There'll be lots going on with the Olympics. I like Vancouver though. I'd stay if I could."

"Something will turn up," Casey said.

They chatted more about jobs.

Finally, Casey stood. "I should be on my way. Thanks again for the coffee."

"Good of you to bring the bickies. Keep in touch."

14

Thursday morning. Casey sat with a coffee in the city hall coffee shop and skimmed the pages of the *Vancouver Sun*.

Margaret Mullen swished in and joined him at his table with a smile. "Good morning, Casey. Okay if I join you?"

She looked fresh and smart in a cream blouse, flowered skirt, silver hoop earrings and black pumps with silver buckles. A faint aroma of freesias surrounded her.

"Hello, Maggie," Casey said. He folded the newspaper and put it aside. "Haven't seen you in a while."

"Been busy," she said. She headed over to the counter and placed her order. Casey watched her, admiring her slim, athletic build. She returned with her green tea.

"You're looking good," Casey said.

"What are you doing Saturday night?" Maggie said.

"You're propositioning me, Maggie?"

"You bet I am. I thought we might go out someplace for that drink we already mentioned."

"I'd like that fine. But I must tell you something. There's already a woman in my life."

Maggie's face registered what, disappointment?

"Is this woman here in Vancouver?"

"She's in Ireland taking care of her mother. She'll be home soon."

"What's her name?"

"Emma."

"What does she do?"

"Teaches school in the West End."

"And you live together."

"No."

"You will let me know if ever you do become an eligible bachelor, won't you?"

"I find it hard to believe there's no permanent man in your life, Maggie."

"There aren't that many interesting and available men out there." She pressed her lips together wistfully.

"That's too bad."

"You better believe it."

"Look, I want to ask you about one of the councilors. You're around them all the time."

"I guess you're still investigating George Nash. Especially now that the police say it's a homicide."

"That's right. Do you know if Angela Brill and George Nash were seeing each other outside of work?"

"You think Angela Brill is involved in Nash's murder?"

"Not necessarily. I just follow leads."

"I don't know a thing about Angela," Maggie said, "except she's always friendly."

As they continued talking, Casey felt something in his brain trying to tell him something. But tell him what? A tiny fact, important but elusive, making it difficult for him to uncover it. And difficult to concentrate on their conversation.

He walked her to the elevator. "I don't have a car. So you want to meet at Cardero's? In Coal Harbor, on the waterfront? I can walk there in ten minutes. It's usually quiet there. We can talk."

"Sounds good," she said.

"Eight all right?"

"Eight it is."

* * *

There had been no rain all morning, only bright sunshine. After his conversation with Mullen at city hall, Casey waited on Cambie Street for a bus to take him back to the West End.

Maggie Mullen still on his mind.

Something niggling at his memory. Bothering him. Something simple and obvious but hiding beyond memory's reach. He knew that this uncertainty had started less than thirty minutes ago, while sitting with Maggie in the coffee shop.

Something to do with Maggie? Something to do with her boldness, how she had asked him out for a drink? Or something else? What?

It was worrying him again now, like an irritating blister on his heel.

He boarded his bus for the West End.

* * *

He hadn't noticed it before, but, in the angled lighting of Cardero's lounge, he could see that Maggie Mullen had faint dimples in her cheeks.

They were sitting in a booth, Casey with an Irish whiskey on the rocks, Maggie with a Hemingway daiquiri. The place was quiet.

Maggie looked good. Dark hair loose to her shoulders, pink short-sleeved top with Peter Pan collar and simple silver heart necklace, silver heart earrings, blue jeans, tan boots with fur round the tops.

Casey wore a casual dark jacket, dark slacks and black loafers, one of the new outfits Emma had helped him pick out before they went away.

"You look nice, Maggie," Casey said.

"Thanks. This is what I wear on friendship dates."

"Brilliant."

"What else do you do besides work for the *Clarion* and make a nuisance of yourself asking questions?"

"Not much," Casey said. "Live a simple life. Enjoy my job." He held up his glass. "I like to drink whiskey. Don't smoke. Jog, work out a few times a week. That's about it."

"That's your life story?" Maggie said.

Casey shrugged.

"You're an uncomplicated man, in other words."

"That'd be me."

"You don't even make long speeches. Most of the men I meet start talking about themselves and then forget to stop."

"What about you?"

"Finished high school. Got a job in a real-estate office. Eventually got myself the council secretary job. Not high profile but pays well. A meteoric rise based mainly on my fertile brain, not to mention my fresh good looks."

"I like your fertile brain and fresh good looks," Casey said.

Maggie smiled.

Casey said, "Your mother didn't remarry?"

"Once was enough for her."

"It must have been tough going."

"Yes, I think so, for my mother. Life is hard for a single parent. I know that now. There was never a lot of money, but we were happy."

They talked together for an hour or so. Then Casey said, "Mind if I ask you a question or two about city hall?"

Maggie made a face. "So that's why we're here? And there's me thinking it was because of irresistible me."

"That too," Casey said.

Maggie smiled. "So what's up?"

She had a beautiful smile. Dimples appeared deeper. Teeth white and even.

"Wait. I already talked too much," Casey said. "I really don't want to ask questions and spoil the evening by talking shop. I'll walk you back to your car."

"We still have lots of other stuff to talk about. We could go back to your place for a nightcap."

"Thanks, Maggie. It's a nice idea, but..."

"You're waiting for Emma."

Casey nodded.

"Why is it," she joked, "that whenever I find a man I like, it turns out he's got principles?"

15

"Casey, it's Emma."

The connection was poor.

"Emma, where are you?" Casey said. "You still in Dublin?"

"I'm stuck here. All flights are canceled because of the ash cloud."

"Not a good line," Casey said. "Canceled because of what?"

"Ash cloud. There's an ash cloud six miles high. Airplanes can't get in or out."

"I hear you. Sorry. The ash cloud. Of course. I should have realized. It's in all the papers. What are they advising people to do?"

"Well, they think air traffic will be stopped for at least three days. Which means I'll miss my connection at Heathrow. I'll be stuck there for a further few days until I can get another flight."

"What will you do in the meantime?"

"I'll stay at a hotel here in Dublin until everything's sorted. Oh, Casey, I'll be so happy to get home to see your ugly mug. How are you anyway?"

"Same old me. Plodding along. I went out for a drink with a woman I met at city hall."

"Who is she?"

"She's the city council secretary. Margaret Mullen. Born here but Irish background. Easy to talk to."

"What did you do after the drink?"

"Went home to bed."

"Alone?"

"Of course alone. You're the only one, Emma."

"Are you sure?"

"Stay safe. I miss you, girl."

After he hung up he reached for his whiskey and soda. His first that day.

* * *

Monday morning. As usual. Casey waited for a bus on Cambie Street to take him back down the hill from city hall to the West End. Maggie Mullen was on his mind again.

He was thinking back to that glitch in his memory, that niggle. Trying to tell him something. It had been after coffee with Mullen at the city hall. Irritating. Like a blister on his heel, he remembered thinking.

A strong breeze came up from Broadway. He pulled on his cap. A young office worker joined him, head bent as she texted on her iPhone. When the bus came, the still-texting young woman stepped on ahead of Casey and stood waiting for a ticket. Casey stood on the sidewalk, eyes level with her shoes. Black pumps.

Why were so many young people texting in public these days as they—?

Black shoes!

That was when it hit him. The buried memory. The blister on his heel.

Maggie's shoes.

Black pumps with silver buckles.

The ones she had been wearing in the city hall coffee shop last Thursday.

Shoes that looked a lot like the shoes of the person on the Shangri-La security tape. The one who had moved in and out of George Nash's apartment on the evening he was murdered. The killer. He or she had been wearing shoes that had buckles of some sort.

He needed to check that tape again to be sure.

Be sure that the shoes were not like the ones Maggie Mullen had been wearing.

The possibility of Maggie Mullen being a murderer was, of course, absurd.

*　*　*

When the Shangri-La security guard saw Casey, he groaned.

"I brought you something, Anthony." Casey handed the guard a brown-paper bag containing a mickey of whiskey.

"I need a few more minutes on that tape, if you wouldn't mind getting it out for me."

Anthony loaded the VCR and left him to it.

It didn't take long for Casey to find the two places on the tape: woman entering apartment; woman leaving apartment. He'd brought a magnifying glass with him. Though the tape was in black-and-white, he could clearly see the square buckles on the woman's shoes. He wondered why he hadn't noticed them before. They reflected light—probably silver—exactly like the ones on Maggie Mullen's shoes.

He thanked Anthony and left.

How many women wore shoes with square silver buckles?

He checked out a couple of women's shoe shops in the downtown.

"You don't see buckles much these days, especially that big," one store manager told him.

"Women are more likely to go for bows. Or more intricate designs, like this," said another manager, showing Casey a shoe with clasped hands in silver. "Or this." He produced a pair of pumps with tiny gold-colored handcuffs on the instep.

Casey nodded his thanks. "You have been a big help."

* * *

"Sorry to be dropping in on you again so soon, Parker," Casey said.

Pauline Parker, her young face smiling. "Not at all. I'm starved for company, not to mention whatever you've got in that little bag."

"Blueberry-lemon cake," Casey said.

"Ooh lovely! Come on in. I made fresh coffee soon as you called."

Casey made himself at home in the chair that could have belonged to Elvis Presley's mother.

Blueberry-lemon, the perfect coffee cake. In small quantities.

Parker collapsed herself onto the rug in her usual yoga position. "Before you start with the questions, Casey, I have news. First, the police paid me a visit on Thursday. Inspector Plink—"

"Plank."

"Plank, Plunk, Plonk, whatever, and another plainclothes man. Thompson, I think his name was. So many questions!"

"Well, they're professionals," Casey said. "Sure to have more questions."

"My good news is they're taking me on again at city hall. In the licensing department."

"Brilliant. I'm happy for you, Parker."

"Thanks. So what's up?"

"I asked about Angela Brill last time. But I didn't ask you if there were any other women visiting Nash in his office."

"Not really. Only that council secretary woman—what's-her-name. Mullen."

"Margaret Mullen?"

"That's the one. Didn't like me."

"How often did you see her?" Casey said.

"Too often. Came in probably once a day to see Nash, usually in the afternoon."

Parker poured Casey more coffee. "Have some more cake."

"No, thanks. Unlike you, I've got to watch my waistline. Why do you think she didn't like you?"

"No idea. Just gave me these dirty looks. Eyes like daggers."

"What did Nash and Mullen talk about when they were in his office?" Casey said.

"Dunno. Nash kept the door closed."

"You think they might've had something going on between them?"

"An affair, you mean? I wouldn't know. They were cool with each other when I was around.

But they could've been covering up. I checked her out. Split with her husband and three-year-old kid about the same time she started working at city hall. Ten or eleven years ago. What kind of mother does that?"

Casey's mind reeled. "What do you mean, you checked her out?"

"City employee records and—"

"You had access to employee records?"

"No. But hacking into the city data bank is simple." Parker waved a hand. "Nothing to it. They know zilch about security. Also, I asked around. Some of the older women remember that she abandoned her little boy. She's been at city hall a long time. Lots of people know her. Mullen is her maiden name."

Casey couldn't believe what he was hearing. Parker's Maggie Mullen was a completely different woman from the one Casey knew.

"Do you remember her husband's name or where he lives?"

"Afraid not."

"Thanks, Parker," Casey said. "You've been an enormous help."

As he was leaving, he said, "I'll keep in touch, Parker. Besides, I'd like to know how that new job of yours works out."

"Lovely," Parker said with a radiant smile. "Thanks for the cake."

* * *

Back at the office, Casey reported his Pauline Parker conversation to Ozeroff.

"Mullen walked out on her husband and kid?" Ozeroff said.

"That's according to the gossip," Casey said. "Who knows what really happened so long ago?"

"And Mullen told you she hardly knew Nash."

"Right again, Deb."

"What is this Pauline Parker like?" Ozeroff said.

"Nice. Young. I trust her."

"So Maggie Mullen is a liar," Ozeroff said.

"I never thought Maggie would lie to me," Casey said. "But now I'm not so sure."

"Maggie Mullen is a lot like me, right?"

"What do you mean?"

"She's witty and a lot of fun to be with."

"That's right, Deb."

"And she's a real good-looker, right?"

"How did you know?"

"Go figure," Ozeroff said, rolling her eyes.

16

Following Tuesday cop shop, Casey called Ozeroff on his cell. "Hegel's Bagels, Deb. High noon."

The forecast was for light showers. It was already pouring sheets.

First to arrive, Casey ordered a toasted ham-and-cheese bagel and a small Caesar salad.

Ozeroff came in, hung up her dripping raincoat and ordered a garden salad.

They sat at the window counter so they could look out at the rain on Denman and the deserted seawall.

"So what's up, Casey?" Ozeroff said.

"Shoes," Casey said.

"Shoes?" Ozeroff said.

"Women's shoes," Casey said.

He told her about the security tape and Maggie Mullen's square silver buckles.

"Shoes like that very common, d'you think, Deb?"

"Shouldn't think so. Never catch me in them."

"How so?"

"That style went out with the Puritans."

"You never talk much about yourself, Deb. Why's that?"

"Too uninteresting. Who cares?"

"I care," Casey said. "You and Vera happy?"

"We were made for each other. Vera reads nonfiction. I read fiction. So we tell one another stories. Did I tell you I started writing a novel in January?"

"A novel? No, you didn't tell me. I'm impressed, Deb. Nothing uninteresting about that."

"Always wanted to be a real published writer. A novel, not a newspaper column. But I never did anything about it. So come New Year's, I made a resolution. This is the year I start my novel. So I did. I started it. Wish me luck, Casey."

"Good luck, Deb. I look forward to buying a signed copy when it's published."

* * *

His first move once home on Tuesday evening was to mix himself a whiskey and soda.

Then he sat with his feet up and gazed out of his balcony window. Barclay Street was quiet. A light drizzle fell softly. A Beethoven sonata played on his stereo. Across the street, Matty Kayle's ginger tomcat hunted birds in the shadow of the rhododendrons.

Casey pondered the question of Nash's secret mistress and her silver-buckle shoes. On their own they were certainly evidence that Mullen was *possibly* the killer. But was this enough by itself? The answer to that question was a definite no. He would need much more than shoes to support that theory.

But what?

And what about all the indications that Mullen was *not* the killer? Her sweet, friendly and outgoing personality. She was the kind of person who wouldn't kill a fly. The kind of woman completely above suspicion. So why was he bothering to investigate her? To clear her, of course, to get her off the hook.

He finished his drink, got up and showered. He put on his bathrobe and mixed himself another whiskey.

What about Mullen's car? He had seen her on more than one occasion driving out of the city hall parking lot in her shiny new Mini Cooper. What if she had a sugar daddy? What if it was Nash who had given her the car? A gift from a wealthy man to his secret mistress. It wouldn't prove that she killed him, of course. But it would certainly prove their connection.

* * *

Wednesday morning was fine. The rain had stopped during the night, and now the sun was drying up the puddles and lifting Vancouverites' hearts.

The Mini Cooper dealership was the only one in town.

Casey hung around the showroom until he could get the attention of the sales clerk. He was very young. Casey had been watching him for the past thirty minutes. The salesman was tall and thin, with dark, oily hair combed onto his forehead to form a fringe. Casey presented him with a paper on which he had written Margaret Mullen's name and license-plate number.

"My name is Casey of the *West End Clarion*," he said, showing his newspaper ID. "Margaret Mullen did not buy the car. Someone else bought it for her. A gift. I need the buyer's name from your records."

The sales clerk told him that the information was private. "Can't help you, sir. Sorry."

"The name will not be published in my paper," Casey said. "I can promise you that."

"If I gave you that information, sir, I'd be fired."

"It will be in your computer database," Casey said. "No one will know how I got it. Your job will be safe." He slid a twenty-dollar bill over the glass counter at the young man. "Perfectly safe, I promise you."

The clerk shook his head. "Sorry, sir, I couldn't possibly…"

Casey took the twenty back and replaced it with a new one-hundred-dollar bill.

The young man looked about quickly, palmed the bill and pushed it into a trouser pocket. "If you wouldn't mind waiting a minute or two, sir, I'll be right back."

Casey waited.

He soon discovered that his hundred dollars had been well spent.

The buyer of Margaret Mullen's Mini Cooper was Everest Enterprises.

The CEO of Everest Enterprises was George Hamilton Nash.

*   *   *

He found DI Plank shuffling papers in his office.

"Okay, Casey, let me see if I've got this right. First there's the shoes on the videotape. You say you saw her wearing the same kind of shoes. That right?"

"That's right, Frank."

"Unusual shoes. Easy to spot. Silver buckles. Kind of old-fashioned style."

"Right."

DI Plank leaned back in his chair and scratched his thin gray hair. "So tell me again about her car."

"It's a new Mini Cooper," Casey said. "The buyer was Everest Enterprises. Everest Enterprises was owned by George Hamilton Nash."

"So Mullen was probably Nash's mistress," Plank said. "No crime there. Nash bought his girlfriend a car. No crime there either. You think Mullen might've killed him because she was jealous of your witness, Nash's new secretary, Pauline Parker."

"It's possible."

"You've got nothing, Casey. A pair of shoes that may or may not be the ones on the tape. Mullen was his mistress and she got a car out of it. But that doesn't mean she killed him. Being a mistress is not a crime. Look, Casey, I'll look into Mullen as a possible suspect, but the Homicide Department is stretched awful thin right now."

"Joanne Drummond, Nash's partner," Casey said. "How is that investigation going?"

Plank sighed. "The mills of justice grind slowly, Casey. Why don't you take a rest and leave this case to me? Poking your nose into a nest of rats can be big trouble. You're gonna get hurt real bad one of these days, mark my words."

"With my Irish luck? Forget it, Frank."

Plank shook his head wearily. "Close the door on your way out."

17

C asey dropped by Maggie Mullen's office, on the third floor of city hall.

"I need to talk with you, Maggie. I'll buy you a coffee across the street, at City Square."

"Sorry, Casey. Not today. I'm up to my ears in work." She flashed him one of her dimpled smiles. "You sound serious."

"Then how about after work?"

"I'll be working late. Sorry. But I could maybe meet you for a drink later if you like. I'll give you a call or send a text message when I'm free."

"Sounds good," Casey said.

* * *

It was just about lunchtime when he got back to the office.

"No messages," Brenda said.

Ozeroff swiveled around on her chair to greet him. "Hey, Casey. Want to take a hard-working, underpaid journalist to lunch?"

"Don't see why not," Casey said.

They ordered salads. Their seats at Hegel's Bagels window gave them views of Denman Street, Morton Park and English Bay. The sunshine had brought everyone out. Walkers, joggers, cyclists everywhere. West Enders. Tourists. Colorful, crowded humanity.

"Who would want to live anywhere else?" sighed Ozeroff.

"Jack moved away," Casey said. "To Victoria, remember?"

Jack Wexler, their former colleague, now retired.

"Just wait," Ozeroff said. "Boredom will bring him back, you'll see. Anything new and exciting up at Silly Hall?"

"The mayor pledges to end homelessness by 2015."

"Good luck with that. You got to admire the guy for trying. Any news on the Nash case?"

Casey told her about Mullen's Mini Cooper.

"So it looks like she was Nash's regular bedmate, right?"

"Looks that way, Deb. But she doesn't seem the jealous kind. Or the crazy kind. Not the killer, in other words."

"Not a psycho," Ozeroff said. "So scratch her off your list of suspects."

"I don't have a list," Casey said. "The only one I have left is Joanne Drummond, Nash's partner. DI Plank is keeping information on that investigation to himself."

"But what about the silver-buckle shoes?" Ozeroff said, turning her attention away from her bean salad for a moment. "And the lies Mullen told? It seems to me your innocent Maggie Mullen had the opportunity to kill Nash. All you need to add to that is the motive. Opportunity plus motive equals suspect. Did Mullen have a motive?"

"My guess would be Pauline Parker was the motive," Casey said. "Parker said Mullen didn't like her. Parker stole her man. But is jealousy enough as a motive? Beats me."

"Of course it is," Ozeroff said. "That's why it's called the green-eyed monster. Green equals envy. Look at Othello. Jealous of his wife. Kills her. End of story."

"But that's just what it is, a Shakespeare story," Casey said.

"You want real life? Then what about the woman a few years ago who found her husband in bed with his mistress? So she ran over him with her car. Then she ran over his body a few more times just to make sure he was good and dead."

"That true?"

"Sure, it's true," Ozeroff said. "Jealousy is a major killer. Do you remember the woman a few years ago who cut off her husband's penis and threw it—"

"Deb, stop! I've heard enough already."

They went back to watching the activity outside in the street until it was time to go.

"Thanks for lunch, Casey."

"You're worth it, Deb."

* * *

His cell buzzed just after five o'clock. He was in his office. It was Maggie Mullen.

"I could meet you around nine if you're still up for it," she said.

"Nine's fine," Casey said. "Cardero's again?"

"I had trouble finding parking there last time," Maggie said. "Even with my tiny car. Tell you what. Meet me in the Bayshore Hotel lounge. That's close to where you live, right?"

"Five-minute walk."

"Good," Maggie said. "Their parking lot is huge."

"I'll see you there," Casey said.

* * *

Maggie was on time. Casey watched her as she made her way gracefully through the automatic doors and across the opulent lobby. She glided into the carpeted lounge where he was waiting for her. He already had a whiskey and soda on the table in front of him.

He got up to greet her. "Hey, Maggie. Let me take your coat."

Under the brown wool coat she was dressed simply in the brown cardigan, tan shirt, matching skirt and black slip-on pumps she'd worn earlier in the day. Fresh scent of freesias.

"Thanks," Maggie said. "It's the first day of summer, but you'd never know it. I'm glad I wore my coat."

Casey wore his casual dark jacket, dark slacks and black loafers. "I already ordered you a Hemingway, is that all right?"

"Perfect," she said.

They sat in plush chairs, facing one another across the table.

"I also ordered a snacking plate of sushi," Casey said. "Thought you might be hungry."

"You think of everything."

The waiter brought Maggie's cocktail and the sushi plate.

They sipped their drinks and made themselves comfortable. But Casey wasn't comfortable. What was he doing here? How could he ask this woman the personal questions that weighed on his mind? She was George Hamilton Nash's mistress. So what? He liked her. He was sure she had nothing to do with his death.

Maggie leaned toward him, a smile on her lips. "So what's on your mind, Casey?"

"It's this Nash murder." He sipped his whiskey, not sure where to start.

"You found something?"

"I'm not sure."

She waited.

He took a deep breath. "You lied to me, Maggie."

She was indignant. "Lied! What lie?"

"I asked you how well you knew George Nash. You told me you only ever said good morning to him. Yet I now know you visited him frequently in his office."

"Frequently?"

"At least once a day. Behind a closed door."

"I don't know who told you that, Casey— probably that new secretary of his—but it's pure nonsense. I haven't been in Nash's office more than once or twice in all the time I've known him. That little nobody is confusing me with someone else, obviously. Either that or she's a nasty little liar."

"My theory is that Nash was killed by a jealous mistress. A woman he knew from city hall."

"Well, it wasn't me. I didn't know the man. You disappoint me, Casey. I thought you knew me better than that. I thought we were friends." She put her drink down on the table and stared at him.

"Friends? Yes," Casey said. "That's what bothers me." He paused, thinking. He didn't want to mention the silver-buckle shoes. That might be a job better left to the police. "Here's another lie, Maggie. You told me you were never married. Not true. You even have a child."

Indignation turned to anger. Flushed porcelain cheeks, blue eyes flashing, chest puffed like a pigeon's. "It's really none of your business, Casey."

"You're right," he said, "it's not. But why lie about never being married?"

"It's not a lie. You ever hear of privacy? What law says I must reveal myself to every stranger?"

"I was a stranger?"

"Yes, you were—and still are, more or less. I would have told you eventually, I'm sure. Very well. I'll tell you now." She paused to take a large breath. "My husband ran off with another woman and took my baby, my little boy. He left me with nothing."

A young couple sat down at the next table. The woman wore a thick red sweater.

Maggie spoke quietly, looking down at their table. "I don't know where my husband is," she said. "I don't know where my son is. It's like they just disappeared." Her tone became accusing. "You wouldn't know what it's like to lose a child, Casey." Her eyes glistened with tears.

He waited.

"Colin would be thirteen now. I haven't seen him since he was three years old. I don't know what he looks like." She fumbled in her purse and took out her wallet. "This is Colin." She handed Casey a snapshot of a small child with bright eyes and a mass of dark curly hair.

Casey studied the picture and then handed it back. "Cute kid."

"I don't know a thing about him," she said. "I don't know whether he's dead or alive." She dabbed at tears with her table napkin. "For ten years I've grieved for my lost baby."

"I'm sorry," Casey said.

"If you think I had anything to do with Nash's death, you're crazy."

"I don't think you had anything to do with his death," Casey said. "I find it impossible to see you as a murderer. I just want to hear you tell me it's not true. Tell me it's not true, Maggie."

"It's not true."

"And you did not have an affair with Nash?"

"No."

"There's one more thing, Maggie. I made inquiries about your car."

"My car? What has my car got to do with anything?"

"Wasn't your Mini Cooper car a gift from Nash? A gift from a rich man to his mistress? A man you say you didn't know? A man you say you had no affair with?"

She glared at him. "I bought the car with my own money. I paid for it, every penny."

"And you weren't Nash's longtime mistress? Tell me the truth, Maggie. Imagine all the questions the police would ask you. They'd ask, 'Did Nash promise to marry you after he left his wife? When he started sleeping with his secretary, were you jealous? He forgot about you. Were you angry? Were you mad, Ms. Mullen? So mad with jealousy that you killed him?'"

Her face was white. "I didn't kill him."

Casey said nothing more.

So far, neither of them had touched the sushi.

"You like me, Casey. I know you like me. How can you...?" Her voice choked with emotion.

She stood, picked up her purse and hurried away toward the washroom.

He watched her go.

It took awhile, but eventually she came back.

She sat down, took a deep breath and looked him in the eye.

"Here's the truth, Casey," she said, cool and composed. No sign of tears. "I was Nash's girlfriend. Sexual partners, if you like. We slept together, but I was not his mistress." She pressed her lips together. "For two years I was his girlfriend. He said he planned to divorce his wife and marry me. So you were right. I lied to you, but I don't apologize for that. My life is my own. It's private. Who do you think you are to come snooping into my life? To accuse me of murder! Some friend you turned out to be!"

Casey said nothing.

"I didn't love George Nash," Maggie said, "but I liked him. He treated me well. So now you know the truth." She sat rigidly, back straight. "But I didn't kill him. I don't know who did kill him, but it wasn't me. You were right about the car too. It was a gift. That's all, just a gift. Why shouldn't I let him buy me a gift? It was nothing to him, with all his money. I was looking out for myself. I grew up with nothing, remember? I was good to George Nash and he was good to me. That's all. It's as simple as that."

"Okay, Maggie, I believe you," Casey said. "I'm sorry. But the police could be asking all these questions and more."

"If you go to the police with what you know, they will make it hard for me," Maggie said. "I want you to tell them nothing. I want you to promise me. I want you to respect my privacy."

"I can't promise that, Maggie."

She glared at him. "Then you're no friend of mine." She stood and retrieved her coat from the back of her chair. He stood to help her, but she marched off quickly across the lobby and out the automatic doors.

He watched her go, then sat and sipped his whiskey.

He didn't know what to think of her. Was she sincere? Or had he just seen a brilliant piece of acting? And heard more of her lies?

Maggie Mullen was either innocent of any crime. Or she was the mother of all liars.

He took out his cell and placed a call to DI Plank.

18

The sushi still untouched, Casey paid the bill and headed out the door.

Almost dark. Twilight of the gods.

The doorman stood outside at the curb. "Taxi, sir?"

"No, thanks," Casey said, crossing the parking lot. He walked past the line of waiting taxi-cabs, their drivers half asleep. Then a row of ornamental trees. Then he was aware of someone behind him. He whirled around but was too late. His head exploded. In the split second that it took to sink into darkness, he saw the sweet, pretty face of Maggie Mullen.

* * *

"What hospital is this?"

"St. Paul's," the nurse said.

"What happened?"

"You have a mild concussion."

Casey pushed himself up on his pillows and raised his arms. He could feel a dressing on the top of his head.

"There's a visitor to see you," the nurse said.

It was DI Plank. He carried a pineapple. He looked uncomfortable. "Can't say I'm surprised to find you in hospital, Casey," he said. "I warned you, remember?"

"What hit me?"

"A Mini Cooper tire iron. In the hands of your friend, Maggie Mullen."

"Thanks for the pineapple."

"Fruit helps the mending, they say." He placed the pineapple on the bedside table. Then he took off his coat and sat in the plastic chair beside the bed.

The nurse picked up the pineapple. "I'll cut some of it up for you," she said, leaving the room.

"It was Mullen," Casey said.

"We know," Plank said. "We got her. You made enough noise to alert the taxi drivers. They held her and called nine-one-one."

"How is she?" Casey said.

"Mullen? She's in custody," Plank said.

"How long have I been here?"

Plank looked at his watch. "Since ten thirty last night. It's now almost ten thirty in the morning. Twelve hours."

"The poor woman had her baby stolen away from her. She was crazy." Casey felt sleepy.

The nurse came in with the sliced pineapple on a plate. "The patient should rest."

Casey said, "She didn't seem crazy. I liked her. Liked her a lot. When can I see her?"

Plank stood and reached for his coat. "Not until we've got her statement and the prosecutor gives the okay. Be a few days. We searched her place. Got the shoes. Got the hoodie. Looks like it's got blood on it. DNA could tie it to the murder scene." Plank put on his coat. "Gotta go." He looked at the nurse. "You keeping him here awhile?"

"We'll see how he is this afternoon," the nurse said.

"I gotta be out of here this afternoon," Casey said. "There's somewhere I need to be."

19

She emerged from customs into the waiting area, dragging her wheeled suitcase behind her.

Casey spotted her immediately and waved.

To Casey, she looked delectable. In beige sandals, blue jeans, pink shirt and white cotton sweater.

She saw him.

"Casey!" she cried, releasing her suitcase and throwing herself at him. "You'll never know how much I've missed that ugly mug of yours. Hey! You look thinner. Did you forget to eat?" She stood back to take a longer look. Her face fell. "What's that bandage on your head?"

"I ran into a tire iron. It's just a scratch."

Emma looked horrified. "Someone hit you with a tire iron?"

"Look, I'm fine. I'll explain later. You're as beautiful as ever." Casey gave her an enthusiastic hug and then grabbed her suitcase. They pushed through the crowd together to the SkyTrain platform.

He couldn't stop looking at her.

A train was waiting for them.

They sat in opposite seats, knee to knee, eye to eye.

"You must be tired," Casey said.

"Not now. It's so good to be back," Emma said, smiling. "And to be with the man I love."

"Meaning me?" Casey said.

"Meaning you," Emma said. "Good thing I'm home. Bad things happen to you when I'm not around."

With the pale blue eyes of her Norman-Irish ancestors, her fine dark brown hair and the freckles arching over her nose like a sprinkling of sand, she was even more beautiful than he remembered. Her warm personality engulfed Casey. Here she was, the bringer of light and air and color to his life.

The sun was shining. Outside, as the train raced through the Richmond countryside, trees were in full leaf, thick and verdant, promising a long, green summer.

"Casey, I'm sorry about John Burns. I know I hurt you and for that I'm sorry." She reached across and took his hands in hers. "This is where I want to be."

"I know."

She was back. That was all that mattered.

The train sped smoothly north, high over the Fraser River, toward Vancouver and home.

ACKNOWLEDGMENTS

I owe a debt of gratitude to my editor, Bob Tyrrell, for his valuable suggestions.

A former fingerprint specialist with the Vancouver Police Department, JAMES HENEGHAN has won numerous awards for his books for young readers, including the Sheila A. Egoff Children's Literature Prize three times. His first book for the Rapid Reads series was *Fit to Kill* (2011). James lives in North Vancouver, BC.